THE CASE OF

THE COP
CATCHERS

Also by Terrance Dicks

THE BAKER STREET IRREGULARS IN

THE BAKER STREET IRREGULARS IN

THE CASE OF
THE COP
CATCHERS

TERRANCE DICKS

LODESTAR BOOKS
E.P. DUTTON   NEW YORK

Copyright © 1981 by Terrance Dicks

Library of Congress Cataloging in Publication Data

Dicks, Terrance.
The Baker Street Irregulars in the case of the cop catchers.
SUMMARY: The Baker Street Irregulars have their hands full solving the mysterious disappearance of their friend Detective-Sergeant Day, a jewel theft, a series of truck hijackings, a missing person case, and a traffic violation.
[1. Detective and mystery stories] I. Title.
II. Title: The case of the cop catchers.
PZ7.D5627Co 1982   [Fic]   81-20910
ISBN 0-525-66765-2   AACR2

Published in the United States by E.P. Dutton Publishing Co., Inc., 2 Park Avenue, New York, N.Y. 10016. Published simultaneously in Canada by Clarke, Irwin & Company Limited, Toronto and Vancouver
Editor: Virginia Buckley   Designer: Trish Parcell
Printed in the U.S.A.   First U.S. edition
10 9 8 7 6 5 4 3 2 1

CONTENTS

1 THE DISAPPEARING DETECTIVE

He was driving too fast, of course, when it happened. He had always liked to drive fast, and at this particular moment he was in a mood of triumphant exhilaration. He had taken great risks, and he was about to reap a great reward.

He had turned last-minute disaster into triumph, dodging catastrophe by a hair's breadth. He had tricked and avoided his pursuers, brought his long-planned schemes to a successful conclusion. There was still a little more to do, but by now the worst was over.

A day or two, a week at most, and he would be on his way, a free man, and a millionaire. He could never come back to England, of course—but there were plenty of places where a wealthy man would be asked no questions.

It was late, and the London streets were almost empty. The big car swept along the dark and silent roads, headlights illuminating closed shops and quiet suburban houses, with here and there a light gleaming in an upstairs window.

He rounded a sharp bend in the road, far too fast, and

suddenly disaster struck. There was no crash, no accident, his brakes were good, his driving reflexes superb. . . .

What happened next was no more than a trivial incident, something most drivers could have soon forgotten, paying the minimal penalty gladly, congratulating themselves on a lucky escape.

For this man, at this particular time, it was complete and utter disaster.

When it was all over, he drove on for a few blocks and then parked the car in a quiet side street. He sat for a while, considering possibilities, forming and rejecting plans, until at last he came up with a possible scheme.

It was typical of the man that his plan was a bold one, the kind of thing most people wouldn't even dare to think of, let alone carry out. It was a reckless, dangerous scheme, but it might just save him—if he acted now.

He opened the glove compartment in the dashboard and took out a gun.

It all started one day at the beginning of the summer holidays—the day Dan Robinson went down to the police station to collect his dog, a big black shapeless beast called Baskerville.

Most dog owners are pleased and relieved at the prospect of getting their lost pet back. But not Dan. This was the seventh time he had had to go and collect Baskerville, and since every trip cost him one pound thirty, Dan was getting pretty fed up with it—particularly since Baskerville had never really been lost in the first place.

The trouble was people just didn't realize that Baskerville

was a street dog, as opposed to a house dog. Attempts to keep him shut up in the house when everyone was out had proved a disaster. Baskerville was an active dog, and he didn't care for confinement. Shut him up in the house and he lolloped up and down, knocking over everything breakable, until he was tired. Then he sat down and let out a series of deep crashing barks, interspersed with loud wolflike howls that brought in a flood of complaints from the neighbors.

They'd tried shutting him in the garden, but he simply hurdled the fence, flattened the neighbors' flower beds, leaped over *their* fence, and nipped between the houses and into the street.

Baskerville was a sociable dog; he liked to see a bit of life. Dan's parents both worked, and in term time, when Dan was at school, Baskerville hung around in the street, greeting old friends, both canine and human, chasing the odd cat up a tree, popping in to local shopkeepers in the hope of a cookie or a sweet. (His usual method was to stand in the doorway and bark until they gave him something to go away.)

When he got bored with all this, Baskerville would take himself off for a romp on the local common. But guided by some mysterious canine clock, he was always on the doorstep at a quarter to four, when Dan got home from school. Or nearly always. One day Dan got home to find Baskerville nowhere in sight.

At first he just assumed Baskerville had gone on a longer walk than usual. But when the big dog didn't turn up by suppertime, Dan was really worried. Baskerville loved his food, and though he demolished two platefuls of meat and dog biscuits a day, he always gave a good impression of being half starved whenever suppertime came around. When Dan's father got home and Baskerville was still missing, he suggested calling the police station. Dan did so and was vastly relieved to hear that a big, black lost dog that could only be Baskerville had been brought in that afternoon. If Dan would present himself with his dog license and the fine of one pound thirty, he could have his dog back.

Dan rushed around to the police station at once, where he found Baskerville wolfing up a plate of scraps from the police canteen. Baskerville woofed a welcome, and Dan paid up and took him home. That was the first time.

The second time it happened, he went through the same routine fairly cheerfully, but by the third and fourth it was getting a bit of a bore.

Dan even went so far as to have a specially large dog tag engraved for Baskerville's collar. One side had the family name and address and telephone number, and the other side bore the message THIS DOG IS NOT LOST.

Nevertheless, well-meaning strangers kept on hauling Baskerville off to the police station, and Dan kept on turning up to bail him out.

Thoroughly cheesed off, Dan marched up the steps, across the lobby, and plunked a pound note and three ten-pence pieces in front of the grinning desk sergeant.

"All right," said Dan bitterly. "Here's the ransom money. I reckon whenever things are slack you send some young copper out to nab Baskerville!"

The sergeant turned over the pages of his big ledger. "The animal was found wandering on the Heath by two small children. It attached itself to them, and was obviously lost and distressed," he said solemnly.

"Lost and distressed! The soppy great thing just loves kids, that's all. Loves everyone, come to that— Why didn't the silly little perishers just bring him home? Can't they read?"

The sergeant shook his head sadly. "That's no way to talk about your benefactors."

"My benefactors! Yours, you mean. I've forked out over nine quid for that great furry fool. Next time it happens you can keep him."

The sergeant scooped up Dan's money and put it in a cash box. "You do have a current dog license, I take it?"

Silently Dan fished out the frayed piece of paper from the back pocket of his jeans and handed it over.

The sergeant unfolded it and studied it. "This one's nearly run out. Be sure and renew it, won't you? You'll need it next time!"

"Very funny. It's all right, I'll get him myself. I know the way by now."

He found Baskerville tied up in the police station yard, devouring the remains of an enormous beef bone.

He looked up when he saw Dan, thumped the ground with his tail in welcome, and went back to the bone.

Dan looked reproachfully at him. "All right, are we? Not pining away?"

Baskerville ignored him.

Dan went to untie the rope, and then changed his mind. "All right, stay on and finish your bone. I'll go and say hello to Happy."

Detective-Sergeant Day, Happy for short, was an old friend of Dan. The two had met when Dan and a group of his friends, known locally as the Baker Street Irregulars— after the kids who helped Sherlock Holmes—had scored their first success, the recovery of a stolen painting. The friendship had grown during the Irregulars' involvement in a number of other cases. Indeed, Day's recent promotion to sergeant had come after the capture of a master criminal called the Planner—a case in which Dan and his friends had given the police a good deal of unofficial help.

Leaving Baskerville to his bone, Dan went back into the police station and along the corridor that led to Day's tiny office. Flinging open the door, he said, "Look here, Happy, can't you tell your lads to stop dognapping—" He broke off in astonishment, wondering if he was in the wrong office.

A quick glance around assured him the office was still the same—two huge green filing cabinets, a desk, two chairs, and that was it. It was the man behind the desk who was all wrong. "Happy" Day was a thin, sharp-featured young man with a taste for stylish Italian-cut suits. Like most Criminal Investigation Department men, he was a smart, not to say flashy, dresser.

The man sitting behind Happy's desk was a very different figure, a solid-looking middle-aged man in a dark suit with a sober tie. He wore heavy horn-rimmed spectacles, and the eyes behind them were cold and hard. He seemed to be sorting through the desk. Several drawers were pulled out and a pile of miscellaneous objects cluttered the desk blotter: pens, pencil stubs, notebooks, writing paper, an assortment of forms and other papers, all arranged in orderly piles.

Dan stood staring at him openmouthed. The man looked up and said, "Yes?"

Feeling like a complete idiot, Dan said, "Sorry—I was looking for Detective-Sergeant Day. This is his office, isn't it?"

"Yes. I'm afraid he isn't here."

By now Dan was recovering from his surprise. "I had worked that out," he said gently. "Could you tell me where to find him, please?"

"He's—away, at the moment."

"Can you tell me where?"

A heavy hand fell on Dan's shoulder. "He's gone on his holidays. Spot of unexpected leave."

Dan knew who it was, even before he turned around. Detective-Sergeant Fred Summers, a tough, burly copper of the old school. Currently Day's colleague, Summers had been his superior officer until the younger man's recent promotion, and he didn't much care for the changed relationship. He didn't care for Dan Robinson and the Irregulars, either.

Summers believed kids should be seen and not heard, especially around police stations. "Sorry about this, sir. I'll get rid of him."

Dan grasped Summers' thick wrist in both hands and lifted it from his shoulder. "It's all right, Sergeant Summers, I'll go quietly."

The man behind the desk said, "You know this boy, Sergeant?"

"Name's Dan Robinson, sir. Confederate of Day's. There's a whole gang of them, call themselves the Baker Street Irregulars."

"Ah, yes, the young amateur detectives. I seem to have heard of them."

Something about the man's supercilious tones got up Dan's nose. "You've had plenty of chances."

"I'm sorry?"

"Chances to hear about us. The stolen painting, the Fagin business, the Planner, the Rio Cinema business, and the fake ghosts up at Old Park House. It's all in the files. Why don't you look it up?"

The man stood up. "Perhaps I will. Now, if you'll excuse me, I have work to do. Detective-Sergeant Day may be away for some little while, so the police will have to do without his, and your, valuable assistance for a while."

Summers edged into the office, and shouldered Dan out of the door. "Out," he said briefly.

Dan stood his ground. "If Detective-Sergeant Day is in trouble, I'd like to hear about it."

Summers grabbed Dan's arm, Dan wrenched himself free again, and the man in glasses said, "Wait a moment, Sergeant." He looked keenly at Dan. "What makes you think Day's in trouble?"

"It's pretty obvious, isn't it?"

"Is it? Why?"

Dan began ticking off points on his fingers. "One, this is Day's office and he isn't here. Two, *you're* here, going through his desk."

"I shall be using the office while Sergeant Day is away. I was merely clearing out a few drawers."

"You were searching the drawers, and listing what was inside. Three, there's you."

"What about me?"

"Summers called you 'sir,' so presumably you're an inspector at least."

"Chief inspector, actually. Chief Inspector Brevett. Go on."

"That's an Inns of Court tie you're wearing, so I assume you're a barrister as well as a policeman. And that makes you a high-powered senior officer from one of the legal departments."

The chief inspector looked as if he didn't know whether to be annoyed or amused. "Even so, that hardly adds up to—"

"You haven't heard point four yet. Fred Summers here said I was one of Day's confederates."

"What if he did?"

"That was the giveaway. Coppers have mates, or colleagues. Villains have confederates. So how come Day's suddenly on the other side of the law?"

Chief Inspector Brevett looked at Summers and said ruefully, "I'm beginning to think this young man deserves his reputation."

"He's a bright kid all right," said Summers gloomily. "Too perishing bright if you ask me. Want me to sling him out now, sir?"

The chief inspector shook his head. "I think things have gone a little too far for that. What is it they say, a little knowledge is a dangerous thing? You'd better sit down."

Dan took the rickety wooden chair. "Learning, actually."

"I'm sorry?"

" 'A little learning is a dangerous thing.' Alexander Pope. It's one of those quotations people always get wrong."

"I'll bear it in mind," said the chief inspector. "All right, Sergeant, you can leave this to me."

Summers gave Dan a final threatening glare on principle, and slammed out of the office.

The chief inspector took off his glasses, polished them on a white handkerchief, and put them on again. "As you so astutely surmise, an allegation of misconduct has been made against your friend, Detective-Sergeant Day." He cleared his throat. "There have been recent leakages of information about police investigations—information that would be worth a great deal to certain people. We received an anonymous tip-off that Day was implicated in this leakage. Naturally we had no alternative but to investigate."

"And what did you find?"

"One thousand pounds in used notes, in a safe deposit box, recently opened by Detective-Sergeant Day under a false name."

For a moment Dan sat there stunned. Then he said, "And what does Day say about all this?"

"So far he's said nothing."

"Then why don't you ask him?"

The chief inspector took off his already gleaming glasses and gave them another polish. "Believe me we should like to—but we've had no opportunity."

"What's that supposed to mean?"

"On the day we received the anonymous tip-off, Detective-Sergeant Day disappeared."

2 THE FRAME-UP

Dan stared at the chief inspector, reeling under the effect of this second shock. "When did all this happen?"

"Yesterday."

"And when you say disappeared—"

"I mean disappeared. He was due to report for duty yesterday morning. He didn't. According to his landlady, he came home late off duty the day before yesterday, got a telephone call just before midnight, went out, and was never seen again!"

Day lodged with a family called Hoskins a few streets away from the station. They'd lost a son in a motorbike accident some years ago, and Day had become a kind of substitute. Dan had met Mrs. Hoskins once or twice, a plump, motherly woman who worried about Day's skinniness, tried to stoke him up with good stodgy puddings, and nagged him constantly about his late hours, his flashy taste in clothes, and the unsuitability of his girl friends.

Day always said he didn't mind the nagging, it reminded

him of home. "It may not be 221B Baker Street, young Robinson, but it suits me."

Dan brought his mind back to the present. "And when did you get this tip-off?"

"Yesterday afternoon."

"*After* he disappeared?" said Dan. "Isn't that odd?"

"Not necessarily. He might have realized someone was going to turn him in—presumably the phone call was a warning from some associate—and beaten them to it by making a run for it first."

"You're talking as if he was proved guilty already."

"Not at all," said the chief inspector huffily. "Detective-Sergeant Day will be given every opportunity to explain himself—if we can find him."

That was it, thought Dan; it was the disappearance that was so damning. What was it they said? "The absent are always guilty." Which made it all the more essential to find Happy. "This safe-deposit box—if it was in a false name, how do you know Day opened it?"

"The box was where the tip-off said it would be—under the name of Henry Dean, in a safe-deposit vault in the city. The manager even recognized Day from our description."

"Was there anything of his actually in the box? Anything with his name on?"

"There was the money and a forged passport in the name of Dean—with Day's photograph inside. Presumably he thought we'd be on to the box, and was scared to go to it. He may have others."

There it was again, thought, Dan, the unthinking assumption that Day was guilty. He supposed it was natural enough. The police hated any hint of corruption in their own ranks. That was why they clung jealously to the privilege of investigating it themselves, to keep it as quiet as possible. And their investigations were ruthless. Dan knew that the danger was not that Day would be treated leniently. On the contrary, he would probably be treated much more harshly than the average member of the public.

The chief inspector stood up. "You realize why I'm telling you all this, I hope?"

"To shut me up," said Dan bluntly.

"Exactly. Since you'd already deduced so much, I thought it wiser to tell you the rest. At the moment we're managing to keep things very quiet. We're letting Day's landlady think he's been sent off on a case. Since he's an orphan, there are no close relatives to kick up a fuss. That only leaves his friends—like you. I'm sure you realize that it's better all around if we clear this up quickly and quietly. Any gossip or publicity could only harm his case."

Dan stood up too. "You needn't worry, I'm not going to go rushing around to the papers. I don't intend to do anything that might harm Day."

The chief inspector seemed satisfied. He showed Dan out, promising to let him know if there was any news, obviously pleased to be rid of him.

Dan went out to the yard to collect Baskerville, thinking that if the chief inspector had taken his remarks as a promise not to interfere, that was his lookout. Dan had promised not to harm his friend, but he hadn't said anything about not helping him.

As he walked back down High Street, Baskerville

lolloping at his heels, Dan was becoming more and more certain of one thing—Day had to be found, and soon.

He bumped into something solid, murmured an abstracted "Sorry," and found that the something had moved in front of him, blocking his path.

" 'Oy, Dan. Wake up!"

Dan looked up and realized that the something solid was his best friend, a stocky fair-haired boy called Jeff Webster, the second-in-command of the Baker Street Irregulars.

"Sorry, Jeff, I was miles away. I've just been down to the police station and—"

"Don't tell me—someone's stolen the crown jewels, the police are baffled, and Her Majesty has called in Sherlock Robinson."

It was Dan's passion for Sherlock Holmes that had been the inspiration for the Baker Street Irregulars.

"It's worse than that," said Dan gloomily. "Someone's stolen our favorite detective. Come home with me, and I'll tell you all about it."

Jeff finished his mug of tea and said, "Old Happy some kind of crook? Doesn't seem possible."

They were in Dan's room, a long, narrow one at the very top of the tall old house he shared with his parents—Dan was an only child. It was a combination bed-sitting room and study—the study part was an old desk Dan had bagged when his mother bought a new one. He was sitting behind it now, swigging tea, while Jeff stretched out in the battered old armchair.

"I should think it doesn't," said Dan indignantly. "And the reason it doesn't is because it isn't true."

"Can we be sure of that?"

"Oh, come on, Jeff. You know Happy. . . ."

"We all do—but how *well* do we know him? He's helped us on a few cases, and we've helped him, but—" Jeff hesitated. "Well, he's not exactly the saintly type, is he? Fond of a drink, a lad with the girls, bit of a flashy dresser."

"What do you expect? He's a copper, not a vicar. They're not all saints, you know, especially in the CID."

"I know they're not all saints," said Jeff quietly. "That's just the point. There've been quite a few scandals recently. You're always saying how hard the police work, and how little they get paid. What makes you so sure Day didn't get tempted by some easy money?"

For a moment Dan glared angrily at his old friend, then he forced himself to calm down. Jeff in his cautious take-nothing-for-granted way was really doing him a valuable service, acting as Watson to Dan's Sherlock Holmes, forcing him to defend his ideas and theories to a skeptical listener.

Dan finished his tea and sat back, thinking hard. He was completely and utterly sure that Day was innocent of any crime—but why was he so sure?

After a moment he said, "All right, Jeff, it's a reasonable question. Like you said, coppers aren't saints, especially in the CID. They've got to be quick-witted and a bit unscru-pulous—like the villains they have to deal with. The differ-ence is the villains get the money, the flashy cars, and the villas in Majorca. The CID are overworked and underpaid, and they have to mix with crooks so they can catch them. And when people in that position find they can make a few hundred, or even thousand, maybe just by letting something slip, or turning a blind eye—well *someone's* going to be tempted."

"But not Day?"

"No. Not Day."

"Why not?"

Dan struggled to express his feelings. "Because he's, I don't know—dedicated."

"To punishing the evildoers and stamping out crime—like Batman?"

Dan grinned, thinking of Day in tights, cloak, and mask. "Well, not exactly. Take your dad, Jeff."

"What's he got to do with it?"

"You know the way he feels about that bank. If he got the chance of clearing off to South America with a fortune, do you think he'd take it? Leave the bank, and his gardening, and his do-it-yourself projects and sit on some sunny hotel beach, surrounded by señoritas?"

Jeff grinned at this unlikely picture. "He'd hate it. He's bad enough when we have our fortnight at Eastbourne. Spends the whole time convincing himself the bank's going bust, the garden's blighted, and the house is falling down, because he's not there to keep an eye on them."

"Exactly. And that's how Day feels about being a detective. He loves it; it's his whole life. He's a natural-born bloodhound, a sort of human ferret. I don't think there's a bribe big enough to make him give it up."

Jeff sat thinking for a moment, then nodded decisively.

"All right, I'm sold. If you're that sure, then I'm sure as well. What do we do now?"

"Find him, of course!"

Jeff's cautious streak came rapidly to the fore again. "Hadn't we better let the police handle that?"

Dan shook his head. "I don't think we can afford to. Something tells me they won't be looking all that hard."

There was a ringing at the doorbell and a chorus of welcoming barks from Baskerville.

Dan went over to the window and peered out. Two figures were standing on the doorstep, a tall thin girl with straight fair hair and a small skinny boy with close-cropped brown hair and ears that stuck out like jug handles—Prince Charles ears, their owner proudly called them. He looked up and let out a bellow that rattled the windowpanes. "Come on, Robbo, we know you're in there. Let us in!"

The rest of the Irregulars had arrived, Liz Spencer and Mickey Denning. Somehow it seemed like a good omen. Dan went to let them in.

Sometime later they were all sitting in the kitchen eating cookies and drinking tea. Mickey automatically assumed that any visit anywhere involved the offer of refreshments, and the others usually managed to find room for a little something as well. Dan had gone through the whole story of Day's disappearance for the benefit of the newcomers. To his relief, Liz had accepted the idea of Day's innocence without question. Dan didn't want to go through that business with Jeff again.

Mickey was equally convinced Day was innocent. Unfortunately, he was also convinced that by now their friend was beyond all help. "We'd better start checking the car wreckers, Dan, and the building sites. Oh, and the motorways as well. Motorway extensions are a big favorite."

Liz looked at him in horror. "I'll probably regret asking this question—but exactly what is going through your gruesome little mind?"

Mickey snatched the last cookie from under Jeff's nose and said loftily, "Oh, come on now, it's obvious what's happened. Poor old Day got in the way of Mr. Big, and he's been taken for a ride. He'll be in the trunk of a car that's been crushed to a cubic foot of steel by now, either that or in the foundations of a new office block. Happens all the time."

"Or maybe he's in seventeen different parcels in left-luggage offices all over London," suggested Jeff satirically. "Of all the bloodthirsty little perishers—" He aimed a cuff at Mickey's head, and Mickey promptly retaliated with a wild swing in the general direction of Jeff's ear. Luckily for everyone he overbalanced and fell off his chair, and Baskerville jumped on top of him, barking delightedly.

It was quite a few minutes before order was restored, and when everyone was sitting down again, Dan said, "All the same, I think Mickey's got something."

Liz paled. "You don't really think that poor Day's been—"

"No, no," said Dan hastily. "I didn't mean about the gruesome bit. I meant the bit about Day getting in someone's way."

"How do you work that out?" asked Jeff, reluctant to believe that any of Mickey's ideas made sense.

"We're taking it that Day's innocent, right?" said

Dan. "Then in that case he didn't disappear voluntarily."

"He could be working under cover."

"Without telling anyone—even his bosses?" Dan was skeptical. "If it had just been the disappearance, I suppose that might be possible. But the disappearance *and* the frame-up suggest someone wants him out of the way—the frame-up with the safe-deposit was to give the police a reason for the disappearance."

"So he's either been kidnapped, or killed."

"That's right—and we'll just have to hope that it's kidnapped. It's a lot more likely anyway. People don't actually knock each other off quite as casually as Mickey thinks, and it'd take a pretty ruthless criminal to murder a policeman. No, I reckon Day must have come across some information that makes him dangerous to someone, and that someone wants him out of the way."

"Maybe he found out about plans for some really big robbery, like the London Airport bullion job, and they want him out of the way till the job's been pulled," said Mickey excitedly.

Dan nodded. "It'd have to be something pretty big to make them take the risk of kidnapping—not to mention the thousand quid they chucked in just for window dressing."

Jeff was working through the problem in his usual dogged way. "So—to find the people who've got Day, we've got to find out whatever *he* found out?"

"That's right."

"And how do we do that?"

"Simple," said Dan. "How do you reckon Day came across this bit of information?"

"Just in the course of his job, I suppose. Maybe he was investigating one crime and it led him to another."

"That's right. So all we've got to do is find out what cases Day was working on."

"And how do we do that?"

"Well, we could try going around and asking at the police station—but I very much doubt if they'd tell us. That chief inspector made it very clear he didn't want any interference. Fred Summers won't help; he never cared for us much anyway."

Mickey was shocked by such ingratitude. "After all we've done for the local coppers, you'd think they'd show a bit more appreciation, wouldn't you?"

"Not in this case," said Dan. "This is the sort of thing where they *really* hate outsiders' being involved."

"Why this one specially?"

"Because of that business about Day's secret hoard of money, you young idiot," said Jeff.

"I see what you mean," said Liz. "They must be feeling very embarrassed about that, to put it mildly. Come to think of it, I'm feeling pretty embarrassed about it myself."

"I'm not," said Dan. "It happens to be one of the most hopeful and helpful things about the case."

"Why hopeful?"

"Well, it's largely the money that makes me think Mickey's gruesome theories are all wrong."

Mickey was stung. "Oh, yeah? How do you make that out?"

"We're starting from the assumption that Happy's innocent, right? He isn't a corrupt copper who's disappeared because he was afraid he'd been found out?"

The Irregulars all nodded and Dan went on, "In that case the money was planted to smear his character—and why bother to smear someone who's already dead?"

"Why bother to smear him anyway?" asked Jeff.

There was something like admiration in Dan's voice. "That's the cunning of it. It gives a reason for Happy's disappearance—and it does something else as well."

"What's that?"

"It takes a lot of drive out of the police investigation."

"How do you make that out?"

"Look, if the police think Day's been kidnapped or murdered, they'll pull out all the stops, set up a big nationwide hunt. They won't rest until they find the people responsible. But if they're hunting for one of their own, a policeman gone bad . . . how much do you think they really want to find him?"

"You mean they'd let him off?" asked Liz.

"Not so much that, though Day's got a lot of friends. Even if he'd gone wrong, they wouldn't be that keen to see him behind bars. But I was thinking of something else. If Day's guilty, *and he's caught*, there'd *have* to be a trial—and a lot of bad publicity for the police. *Wouldn't* it be better for everyone if he quietly disappeared?"

"I see what you mean," said Jeff. "You said it was helpful, as well as hopeful."

"It is. It tells us quite a lot about the man we're looking for. Someone with brains, who understands human nature. Someone with plenty of nerve, who doesn't mind committing a serious crime to cover up another. And it tells us another thing—there's really big money involved. Anyone who can throw away a thousand quid just for window dressing. . . ."

"You sound almost as if you admired him."

Dan grinned. "Maybe I do. But I'm going to catch him all the same—or rather, we are."

Mickey was hopping up and down with impatience. "Let's get on with it then. Where do we start?"

"We begin at the beginning. With Mrs. Hoskins, Day's landlady . . ."

3 THE CLUE

Mrs. Hoskins stared in astonishment at the four kids crowding her doorstep.

She recognized one of them—the tall, thin boy at the front of the little group. "Hello, Dan! If you've come to see Mr. Day, I'm afraid he's gone away."

"I know," said Dan quietly. "Do you think we could come in for a moment?"

Mrs. Hoskins was puzzled but friendly. "Yes, of course. Come into the kitchen. I'm just making a cake." Mrs. Hoskins was the sort of woman who was always just making a cake, that or an apple pie or a steak pudding.

When they were all sitting around the Formica-topped table in the little kitchen, Dan said, "I don't want to alarm you, Mrs. Hoskins, but we're a bit worried about Happy."

"I knew it. I knew there was something wrong!"

"What makes you say that?"

"He comes home late from work, gets this midnight phone call, goes out, and just doesn't come back. No phone

29

call, no message, nothing! I mean I know he has to work all hours, but he's always been very considerate, always found time to ring up if he wasn't coming back for his supper. There's many a meal I've cooked that's dried up in the oven waiting for him, but he always let me know. Then there was those policemen."

"What policemen?"

"That Fred Summers, from down at the station. Surly brute he is. Brought another one with him, tall man with glasses, very well spoken. Chief-Inspector Brevett . . ."

"What did they tell you?" asked Liz.

"They said he'd been sent off on some special job, all very hush-hush. I was to carry on as usual, tell anyone who asked he was away on leave, and he'd get in touch as soon as he could." Mrs. Hoskins looked anxiously at them. "*Has* something happened to him, something they're not telling me?"

"We don't know," said Dan quietly. "But we intend to find out. And you could help us."

Mrs. Hoskins was more than ready to help in any way she could, and it took Dan quite a while to reassure her and calm her down enough to answer his questions.

No, Day hadn't seemed worried about anything before his disappearance. He'd been his usual self, overworked, grumbling, but basically quite cheerful about it.

"Was he worried about money?" asked Dan. "Hard up, in debt, anything like that?"

"Well, he was never exactly rolling in it," said Mrs. Hoskins. "Still, it was better since the promotion, and he was always very careful, rent paid promptly at the beginning of the month."

"Did he seem especially *well* off lately?" asked Jeff. "New clothes or a new car, anything like that?"

"Not on what they paid him. Considering the hours he worked, it's a fair disgrace—even since the promotion it wasn't exactly a fortune."

Dan's further questions failed to produce anything useful. There was no sign that Day had been anything but his usual cheerful, hardworking self in the weeks or even months before his disappearance.

"Do you think we could have a look at his room?" asked Dan at last.

Mrs. Hoskins led them upstairs to the front bedroom that had been converted into Day's bed-sitting room. As soon as he took a look around the room, Dan knew they were wasting their time. The place was just too tidy. Day might not have much in common with Dan's fictional hero Sherlock Holmes, but he did share one characteristic with the Great Detective. For all his personal neatness, Day was quite amazingly scruffy at home. Maybe he didn't exactly keep his cigars in the coal scuttle and his tobacco in the toe of an old Persian slipper, but that was probably just because he didn't smoke. Nor did he keep his unanswered correspondence transfixed to the mantelpiece with a jackknife, or write the Queen's initials on the wall in bullet holes, but then again, Mrs. Hoskins wouldn't have stood for it.

What he did do was keep the room covered with a fine old litter of socks, used coffee cups, out-of-date newspapers. He hung up his used clothes on the floor, and his official papers, like those of Sherlock Holmes, were usually scattered all over the room.

But not today. The room was spotlessly clean and immaculately tidy, with no trace of Day's presence at all. Dan looked at Mrs. Hoskins. "Been having a bit of a cleanup, I see."

"Well, they left the place in such a mess."

"Who did?"

"Those other policemen. They said there were things here Day needed for his work, and they had to get them to him. I don't know what they were after, but they went right through the whole place. So I thought I might as well get the place clean and tidy, for when he came back."

Jeff looked around the room. "Do you want to see if they missed anything, Dan?"

"Not after a full-scale police search. Anyway, Brevett didn't look like the kind of man who'd miss anything."

Mickey had been unusually silent all this time, but he was thinking hard. Suddenly he said, "Did he ever use any other room, Mrs. Hoskins?"

"Well, not really. He usually had his meals in the kitchen with the rest of us. He used to sit in the front room now and again, when he wanted a bit of peace and quiet. Said the atmosphere helped him to think."

"Do you think we could take a look?"

Mrs. Hoskins led them downstairs and opened the door of the front room.

The Irregulars stood in the doorway. The room was so neat and tidy they hardly liked to go in.

This was a proper front room, the room with the best furniture, the best carpet, the polished mahogany sideboard, and all the framed family photographs, knickknacks, and souvenirs. The mantelpiece, sideboards, and occasional tables were filled with ornaments, including a set of china Alsatians, a flimsily draped bronze lady holding a torch, a glass jar of multicolored sands, and an assortment of souvenir ashtrays from various seaside resorts.

The thing about this room was that it was never actually used. Everything in it was for "best." It was a kind of museum. Mickey looked around approvingly. He knew all about front rooms; there was one very much like this in his own house. He went straight to the sofa and lifted the heavy seat cushions. Underneath, as he expected, there were neatly piled newspapers, one pile under each cushion.

Mickey went through both stacks and straightened up holding a shabby exercise book, the kind you buy for a few pence in Woolworth's. "What about this, Mrs. Hoskins?"

Mrs. Hoskins took the book from him and leafed through it. The pages were filled with scribbled notes in pencil. "That must be his. It's his writing, anyway, can't read a word of it!"

Dan took the book from her and examined it. "This could be very useful, Mrs. Hoskins. Do you think we could borrow it for a while?"

"I don't see why not, since you're friends of his. . . ."

They said their good-byes and hurried off, promising to let Mrs. Hoskins know as soon as there was any news about Day.

It was only a short walk back to Dan's house, and on the way Liz asked, "How did you know where to look, Mickey?"

Mickey grinned. "Well, I guessed we were looking for papers of some kind, and where else would you look for loose papers? Can't just leave them lying about, can you, not in the *front* room? If you lot were civilized, you'd know that."

Before long they were back in Dan's room, and Liz, Jeff, and Mickey looked on with mounting impatience as Dan studied the book.

Finally Mickey burst out, "Well, come on, then, Robbo, let's have it. Tell me all about my brilliant discovery."

Dan was silent for a moment, and Jeff said, "It's nothing incriminating, is it? Not a list of mysterious financial transactions involving numbered Swiss bank accounts, and things like that?"

"Well, not exactly. But it does reveal one secret that Day wanted to keep quiet about."

"What's that?" asked Liz anxiously.

"His first name!"

"Never knew he had one," said Mickey.

"Well, you don't think he was christened Happy, do you?"

"Don't see why not. There's a kid at school called King."

"And what about all those jazz musicians, like Count Basie and Duke Ellington?" said Jeff.

"There's a girl at school called Patience," said Liz. "And one called Hope as well."

Dan held up his hands. "I know. And in Puritan times people had names like Praise-the-Lord-and-Smite-His-Enemies-Hip-and-Thigh Smith. Nevertheless, Happy, as you all know, is a nickname. Now all is revealed. The *H* in Detective-Sergeant H. Day stands for Herbert—it's written on the front here!"

Mickey gave a hoot of laughter. "No wonder he kept quiet about it. Wait till I see him again!"

"*If* we see him again," said Liz, and Mickey sobered down, remembering the purpose of the investigation.

"Come on, Dan," said Jeff. "What's it all about?"

Dan tapped the scruffy exercise book. "Well, I don't know if you know it, but all detectives have to keep an official notebook, a kind of diary. It records all the progress of an investigation—where they went, who they saw, how many hours on duty, what time they booked in and out. . . . Now the thing is these books often have to be produced in court, especially if the police evidence is challenged. So every good copper makes sure his diary is nice and neat and accurate, and ties in with all his colleagues' diaries."

Jeff looked at the scruffy notebook. "If that's it, old Happy wasn't doing so well!"

"Well, it is and it isn't," said Dan. "Remember, CID men are out and about most of the time, and you don't produce nice neat diaries on the bar of a pub or the seat of a car."

"It's a rough book!" said Liz. "He kept a rough notebook while he was actually on the job, and wrote it up all nice and neat when he was back in the office."

"Exactly! Presumably the cops have got the official diary already, and they didn't even bother to look for this one."

"What does it say, Dan?" asked Liz eagerly. "Anything to help explain what happened to him?"

"Well, not on the face of it. It seems to contain details of three cases he was working on: some truck hijackings, a robbery from an office safe, and a disappearance."

Mickey whistled. "Poor old Happy had his hands full, didn't he?"

"It's only in mystery stories that the detective works on

just one case," said Dan. "In real life he spends his time rushing from one case to another in the hope that something will turn up! Quite a lot of robberies never get solved at all simply because the police haven't really got time. I think there's about a twenty-percent success rate in London."

Jeff said, "Well, it's nice to know what old Happy was working on, but I don't see how it's going to help us find him."

"Don't you? Remember what we were saying earlier? Day's been framed and put out of the way because he's learned something someone else wants hidden."

"So?"

"We also agreed that he probably came across the information in the course of his work, right?" Dan tapped the notebook. "There are three crimes listed in here. The rough notes are very rough, Day's handwriting was lousy, and there are bits in a sort of private shorthand, but I think I can make out the main outlines."

"All right, then, let's have it."

Dan bent his head over the book. "Crime one, a series of truck hijackings, which seem to center around a firm called Anderson Transport."

"That's the one," said Mickey instantly. "Plenty of big money in that."

"Crime two, the mysterious disappearance of a local businessman, a Mr. James Fillmore. One of the partners in Fillmore and Patterson, Nursery Gardeners and Garden Suppliers. Went off to work one morning, never seen again."

Liz said, "Well, that could be a major crime. Suppose he was murdered?"

"You could be right," agreed Jeff. "I know Fillmore and Patterson, my dad buys a lot of stuff from them. It's a heck of a big firm, must be worth a lot of money."

"Crime three," said Dan. "The theft of a diamond necklace from Carabosse and Company. There's something scrawled here about 'an impossible crime.' "

"Maybe that's it," said Jeff. "There's your master criminal! You know—a gentleman crook, like Raffles!"

"Is that all there is?" asked Liz.

"Crikey, it's enough, isn't it?" said Mickey. "What more do you want, Jack the Ripper?"

Dan leafed through the book. "There's a scrawled note on the very last page—a car number, a name—Domingues—and something about 'failing to give due precedence.' "

"What does that mean?"

Dan grinned. "Well, if I remember my police terminology, it means not stopping for a pedestrian on a zebra crossing! We can probably ignore that one!"

Liz said, "All right, Dan, so we know what Day was working on before he disappeared. I still don't see how that helps all that much."

Dan spelled it out. "Well, of course it helps. If Day found out whatever made him a menace to someone in the course of his work, then the person behind one of these three crimes must be the kidnapper."

"Or murderer," said Mickey with gloomy relish. Fond as he was of Day, he still couldn't quite abandon the idea of the corpse in the lonely hidden grave.

Liz said, "Let's say you're right. There are at least three major crimes there, four if you count the great zebra-crossing mystery. Even if Day is missing, we can't go around doing his job for him while he's away. I mean, you are not suggesting we try and solve all three of those crimes, are you?"

"Oh, yes, I am," said Dan. "That's exactly what we're going to do!"

4 THREE CRIMES

Jeff stared at Dan openmouthed. "You've come up with some pretty mad schemes in your time, Dan Robinson, but this is the limit. Are you really suggesting that we should take over not one but *three* police investigations?"

"I'm not saying it'll be easy. I'm not even saying it's sensible. But as a plan, there is one thing to be said for it."

"What?"

"It's the only plan we've got! How else are we going to tackle this?"

No one had an answer.

"Right," said Dan, and waved the notebook at them. "There are three cases in here—the truck hijackings, the disappearance of a local businessman, and a diamond necklace taken from an office safe. The thing is, where do we start?"

"Well, which crime is the most likely to be behind Day disappearing?" asked Liz. "That's the one we ought to concentrate on, surely."

39

"I quite agree. But which one is it?"

A heated argument broke out. Liz herself favored the disappearance. "After all, the man could have been murdered, for all we know. And it all seems to fit somehow—one disappearance leading to another."

Jeff reckoned it was the jewel robbery. "Maybe Day was getting too close and they put him out of the way while they made their getaway. Could be part of a whole series of crimes."

Mickey was quite convinced it was the hijacking. "The jewel robbery could be someone in the shop chancing his arm, and the disappearance could be just that," he argued. "Someone losing his memory, or just getting fed up and clearing off. But truck hijacking is big-time professional crime, it'd need a proper gang. And it'd take a gang to have the cheek to kidnap a detective."

Dan sat listening to the debate, without joining in. Finally Jeff said, "All right, Sherlock, which one do you pick?"

"It is a capital mistake to theorize without data," said Dan, in his most Holmesian tones. "Since you're all three so convinced you're right, you can each go and find the evidence to back up your own theories. It'll save the usual wrangle over who does what."

"And what will you be doing, while we're out doing all the work?"

"Thinking," said Dan with immense dignity. He rummaged in his desk and found three pieces of paper and three pencils, passing them around to the three other Irregulars. "All right, then, it's briefing time. You can all get started this afternoon and come back and see me as soon as you've got something to go on."

Mickey looked disgustedly at his pencil and paper. "You mean we've got to take notes? It'll be just like doing homework."

"You need names and addresses and telephone numbers, don't you? You don't want to have to try and remember it all, do you?"

"I suppose not, but—"

"Good, then we'll start with you, Mickey. Ready? A series of truck hijackings, centered around the premises of Anderson Transport Limited. . . . "

"All right, all right, I'm not doing shorthand, you know!" Licking his lips, Mickey stuck out his tongue and began taking laborious notes.

An hour later, after a quick dash home for lunch ("Can't stop, Mum, I'm on a case"), Mickey was chaining his bike to the railings that surrounded the premises of Anderson Transport. It was typical of Mickey that he had formed no plan about how he would carry out his investigations. Instead he was following his usual policy—plunging straight in and seeing what turned up. Something usually did, though not always what he expected.

He began by surveying the layout. Anderson Transport consisted of an enormous parking lot, filled with trucks of all shapes and sizes. To the right of it was a paved yard holding one or two more trucks and several ordinary cars. The yard was surrounded on three sides by buildings. The one directly ahead was long and low and looked like offices

and storerooms. Those on either side were huge and han-
garlike. Huge doors were slid back to reveal workbenches,
more trucks, some of them in various stages of assembly,
and overalled men moving around rows of workbenches.
There was a gatehouse to the right of the open gates, with a
burly uniformed security man sitting inside. For a moment
Mickey's heart sank. He'd had a vague picture in his mind of
some tiny yard with an old truck or two, but this was obviously a big and complex business. Where on earth was he
going to start?

Suddenly, as if in response to some silent signal, the men
at the benches stopped work and disappeared inside the
hangar.

Mickey looked at his new digital watch. It was 13:01—
lunchtime! Even the watchman in the gatehouse ducked
down, presumably getting his sandwiches. For a moment
the yard was deserted, and on a sudden impulse Mickey
dashed inside. Ducking between cars and trucks, he worked
his way toward the little office building.

He was crouched behind the enormous wheel of a giant
truck when a plain black sedan drove into the yard and
parked with a squealing of tires. A familiar bulky figure got
out and headed for the entrance.

Mickey heard excited barks, running footsteps, and a
voice shouting, "Oy! Where do you think you're going?"

The bulky figure swung around. "To see Mr. Anderson.
Don't worry, he's expecting me."

"Not supposed to just drive straight in the yard like that.
Didn't you see the sign?"

"When I drove up, you had your head down gobbling

sandwiches—egg-and-tomato by the state of your uniform —and ogling the pinup on page three of the *Sun*."

"I'll have to have your name. All names to go in the book."

"My name is Detective-Sergeant Summers. I'm here on police business, I've got a little book of my own, and if you don't get out of my way, you'll be in it! Now hop to it, and take Fido with you."

Summers marched into the office, and the discomfited security man went back to his hut, the Alsatian gamboling at his heels.

Mickey crouched down behind his tire, wondering what to do now. Of all the unlucky coincidences—whatever cover story he made up would be blown at once if Summers caught sight of him. Mickey considered giving up and going home. He looked back at the gate, but the security man, obviously needled by Summers' remarks, was marching up and down with aggressive vigilance, the dog beside him. So if he couldn't go back, he'd have to go forward. Waiting till the guard was looking the other way, Mickey dashed toward the office building and ran along the side wall and down the back.

The rear of the single-story building was broken up by three windows, all open. Dropping on hands and knees, Mickey scuttled along, crouching below each window and listening. From the first came the slow *tap-tap-tap* of a typewriter. Mickey peered in and saw a bored-looking brunette with a beehive hairdo. She was typing a letter, apparently one word at a time, pausing between her efforts for a furtive read of a magazine called *Hospital Romances*.

Mickey ducked down again, scurried to the second window, and heard the voice he'd been listening for—Detective-Sergeant Fred Summers, sounding unnaturally polite.

"Yes, I know it's a nuisance, sir, but the officer originally on the case has been—reassigned, and I've had to take over at short notice."

"What are you up to?" grumbled a deep, hoarse voice. "Using me for a police-training exercise? Didn't the other bloke leave you notes or something?"

"Yes, of course, sir, and I've studied them thoroughly. But between you and me, he was a bit inexperienced, and the notes aren't all that full. It'd be a big help to me if you could just go over it all again."

"And an even bigger help to me," thought Mickey. He decided that Summers hadn't bothered to read the notes at all and was blaming Day for his own laziness.

"All right, all *right*," rumbled the other voice, presumably that of Mr. Anderson. Mickey peeped over the sill and got a quick glimpse of a plain, workmanlike office. Behind a desk, his back toward the window, was a beefy, broad-shouldered man in shirt sleeves, with a fringe of iron-gray hair around an otherwise bald head. Summers sat in the visitor's chair opposite. Luckily he was looking down at the folder on his knee, and Mickey ducked out of sight before he was spotted. He sat cross-legged below the window, listening to the low rumble of Mr. Anderson's voice, which sounded not unlike an engine itself. "Well, I'm in trucks, right? You don't have to be a detective to see that. Trucks of all shapes and sizes, from little vans to full-sized containers. I buy 'em, sell 'em, hire them out, repair them—even make the ruddy things. But mostly I lease them out—rent them to other companies who don't want the bother of running their own fleet. They hire from us and the trucks are always there, always working, fully qualified driver guaranteed. They pay a bit over the odds, but they save a lot of time and trouble. I started small, but I've grown big, so now my trucks handle all kinds of stuff, all over the country."

"Very interesting, I'm sure, sir," said Summers in a tone that made it clear that he couldn't have cared less about Anderson's business successes. "Now, about these robberies."

"I'm coming to that. Now in my game, what counts is reputation, right? Well, recently, I've been getting a reputation I could do without. A reputation for being hijacked."

Mickey heard Summers heave a sigh. "Well, a lot of it goes on, sir, we all know that. I mean it's not *just* you."

"Oh, sure, sure, every now and again, you get a load nicked. But there's something funny about these hijackings."

"How do you mean, sir?"

"Well, sort of—selective." Anderson struggled for words. "What I mean is, some loads are more worth nicking than others. One of my trucks might be carrying anything—junk furniture, fruit, machinery, frozen beef, you name it. I mean it's all worth having, but some loads are a lot more worth having than others. Booze, for instance—the last load we lost was a cargo of Scotch whiskey. Or cigarettes . . . a couple of loads of them went recently. Or antiques. We was carrying a mixed load down to the docks, with a few cases of antique silver in it—and that load went. It's always the good stuff, see, things that are easy to sell, really valuable or easy to get rid of. Nobody ever hijacks a truckload of spuds, or a cargo of sausages."

"But are you sure it's not just chance?" persisted Summers. "I mean, you run a big operation, you move a lot of stuff, so more of yours gets nicked—proportionally like."

"Proportionally my—foot!" said Anderson explosively. "Look, it was my insurance company put me on to it. They've got it all worked out statistically. You carry so many loads, you reckon to get so many nicked. You know, like they can tell how many people are going to get run over every year. They don't know which ones, but they've got a rough idea how many. Well, my losses are three times what they ought to be. Much more and they'll refuse to insure me!"

There was a pause, while Summers considered. "So it comes down to inside information, doesn't it, sir? Probably the drivers."

"No!" said Anderson definitely. "When the hijackings began, I started rotating the drivers suddenly at the last minute. Didn't make any difference. Then I started a sealed-orders system. Bloke turns up for work, he doesn't know if he's taking coals to Newcastle or tea to China. Didn't make a scrap of difference."

"It could still be them," argued Summers. "All right, so you don't tell them till the last minute, but you've got to tell them sometime. A quick phone call, a message note chucked from the cab . . . "

"And somebody sets up a full-scale hijack at the last minute? You ought to know better than that, Sergeant. These are professional jobs, decoy signs, getaway vehicles, the lot.

No, somebody knows the right trucks to pick, and they know a lot earlier than ten minutes in advance."

"So, who does have the information—apart from you?"

"Nobody. Nobody at all. *I* check the jobs as they come in, *I* assign the trucks and the drivers." Anderson gave a gloomy chuckle. "Maybe you'd better arrest *me*, Sergeant."

"Is that a confession sir?"

"No, of course it ruddy well isn't! I spent years building this business up, do you think I'd start ruining myself, and then call you in to catch me?"

After a rather embarrassed pause, Summers said, "I suppose there must be a good deal of paperwork, sir—lists and so on? What about your secretary? How long has she been with you?"

"One day! And she'll be gone tomorrow, thank the Lord. I've got an arrangement with all the big temp agencies, new girl every few days. Another bright idea that didn't help."

"What about outsiders, sir? Someone breaking in and getting a look at the lists?"

"All the papers go in that safe every night, and I've got the key. You saw our security man?"

"We had a few words. Tried to stop me getting in here."

"Well, you know how keen he is then. Him and that precious dog of his are patrolling the place day and night. He lives in that house on the corner, never leaves the site. And before you start accusing him, he never lays eyes on the list and wouldn't understand it if he did." Anderson lowered his voice. "Between you and me, he's a bit dim."

"Maybe that's why he's so stroppy," said Summers. He

stood up. "Well, thank you for your cooperation, sir. I'll be on my way."

"Aren't you even going to have a look around?"

"Don't see the point," said Summers frankly. "We seem to have established the information leak isn't here, so we'll have to look somewhere else. I'm still not convinced it's any more than a run of bad luck, but we'll make some inquiries. . . ."

Mr. Anderson blew up. Summers tried to soothe him, and Mickey listened to the ensuing argument in such fascination that he didn't notice someone moving up behind him.

Something cold and wet touched the back of his neck, and he jumped about a foot in the air. Just behind him was the Alsatian, and behind the dog was the burly security man from the gate.

In a low, bloodcurdling voice, the man said, "That's a trained attack dog there, sonny. One word from me and she'll have you. So if I were you, I'd keep very, very still."

5 CAUGHT!

Mickey stared hard at man and dog, sizing them up. It wasn't the first time he'd been surprised by a guard dog; in fact, he'd first met Dan's dog Baskerville in very similar circumstances.

This particular dog was an Alsatian bitch, not yet full grown. She was poised expectantly, staring intently at Mickey. Awaiting the command to spring? Somehow he didn't think so.

Slowly he straightened up, and as he did so, something round and hard nudged against his foot. He looked down and saw a well-chewed rubber ball. Swiftly Mickey bent down, scooped up the ball, and flung it as far as he could. With a joyous bark the dog scampered after it, leaving the security man gaping foolishly.

As the man turned to call the dog back, Mickey prepared to dodge around him and run for it. Then, for the second time in as many minutes, he got the shock of his life. An enormous hand came out of nowhere, grabbed him by the

49

back of his belt, and lifted him bodily off his feet. Kicking and struggling wildly, Mickey was heaved through the open window and dumped on the scruffy coconut matting before Mr. Anderson's desk.

Detective-Sergeant Summers looked down at his captive and groaned. "Oh, no, not you!"

Indignantly Mickey jumped to his feet. "That's assault, that is, Fred Summers. Police brutality! I'll report you to the Home Secretary."

"I'll give you brutality, my lad. You were warned not to interfere. If you're not out of here in five seconds flat—"

Mr. Anderson had been watching them in mingled exasperation and amusement. There was something very comical in the sight of the enormous detective towering over the skinny but defiant intruder. "Hang on a minute, do I take it you know this kid?"

"Of course he knows me," said Mickey cockily. "You might say we were colleagues. Go on, Sergeant, tell him who I am!" Mickey spoke with the modest confidence of Clark Kent about to reveal that he was really Superman.

Summers looked rather shamefacedly at Mr. Anderson. "There's this gang of kids, like to play at being detectives. . . ."

"Play!" yelled Mickey. "Who found that painting then? Who caught Fagin—and the Planner? Who solved that business at the cinema, and those fake hauntings at Old Park House?"

To Mickey's surprise and delight, Mr. Anderson said, "The Baker Street Irregulars, right? I read all about you in the local papers."

"They have had one or two lucky successes," admitted

Summers grudgingly. "But you don't want kids hanging around here bothering you."

"I'll decide what I want, thank you," said Anderson firmly. "Your lot have had this case for about three weeks, and as far as I can see, all you've managed to do is get rid of the detective who's supposed to be solving it. Let's see if these kids can do any better. You willing to have a go, son?"

Mickey nodded eagerly. "That's why I came here, to have a preliminary look around."

"Now look here, Mr. Anderson," protested Summers, "You can't be serious—"

"Is there any law says I can't engage a private inquiry agent?"

"Well, no, but they're just kids—"

"Is there any law says how old the agent has to be?"

Summers was silent. Law had never been his strong point.

Mr. Anderson fished a crumpled pound note from his back pocket. "Here, we'd better make it official!" He handed the money to Mickey. "I hereby engage you to inquire into who's been nicking stuff from my trucks. Money has changed hands, and a binding verbal contract now exists." Solemnly Mr. Anderson and Mickey shook hands.

Mickey pocketed the pound note. "I shall have to ask you to leave me alone with my client, Sergeant," he said grandly. "We wish to confer in confidence."

Summers glared, sputtered, and turned an alarming shade of purple. Then he snatched up his briefcase and marched from the room. They heard the screech of tires as his car roared out of the parking lot.

Mr. Anderson chuckled. Then his face became serious again. "I don't suppose you and your mates can do anything, not really?"

Mickey grinned. "Look, I know you only said all that to get a rise out of old Summers. But there's a good chance we can help, you know. And like you said, we can't do any worse than the cops are doing at the moment. What have you got to lose?"

"What indeed?" said Mr. Anderson gloomily. "All right, where do we start?"

"With me taking a look around, if that's all right with you."

Mr. Anderson jumped up. "Certainly. Take you around myself."

Over the next hour Mickey gained a thorough grounding in the transport business. He walked through the parking lot where rows of colossal vehicles waited like dozing elephants. He walked through echoing workshops, where trucks were being put together, taken apart, their engines repaired, and their wheels realigned. Mr. Anderson took him to a separate annex and showed him a vast metallic spider's web with a truck chassis in its clutches like some great metal fly. "Called an American Bear, that is, only one or two others in the country."

"What does it do?"

"See that truck? It was one of the ones they hijacked—or tried to. Driver crashed the truck, went clear off the motorway. They didn't get a thing! That chassis got twisted, see, in the accident, got to be straightened out again. Now if you heat the metal and do it, it leaves a flaw. Straighten it out cold and it's as good as new." Mr. Anderson pointed. "Those clamps increase the pressure, bit by bit, bending it straight again. It's all controlled from that keyboard." Mickey saw a complicated control setup connected to the machine.

Mr. Anderson introduced Mickey to his foreman, a dour Yorkshireman called Sowery, and told him Mickey was to have the run of the place and ask all the questions he liked.

As they were leaving the workshop, the security man came hurrying across the yard, his dog at his heels. He looked at Mickey in astonishment. "That nosy kid still here, Mr. Anderson? Want me to chuck him out?"

Mr. Anderson led the security man aside. "Certainly not, Mr. Burton. He may look like a nosy kid, but he's really a great detective in disguise. So just you watch out!"

Burton glared suspiciously at Mickey and retreated to his hut.

Mr. Anderson said, "Don't worry about old Dave Burton, he's been with me since I started. We used to be truck drivers together. Takes life very seriously, old Dave." He looked at his watch. "I'll have to leave you to it, me old Sherlock—got a mountain of paperwork waiting."

He turned and hurried back to the office, leaving Mickey alone in the big yard.

A little disconsolately, Mickey watched him go. Up to now things had gone pretty well. He'd managed to thumb his nose at old Fred Summers, and he was even on the case officially.

Mickey looked around at the office, the workshop, the parking lot and the security hut. It was up to him now—and where was he going to start?

Jeff said, "The thing is, Dad, I need some kind of introduction. Since these people are clients of yours . . ."

Mr. Webster looked worriedly at his son. They were in his office at the bank of which he was assistant manager. Unlike Mickey, Jeff believed in making preparations, and it had occurred to him that since Carabosse and Co. were in the same street as his father's bank, there was at least a chance that they had their account there. As it turned out, they had.

But Mr. Webster was very dubious about involving the bank in his son's rather unusual hobby. He was an intensely conventional man, devoted to his bank, his garden, and home do-it-yourself, and he'd always had doubts about Jeff's interest in crime. For one thing, it occasionally brought publicity, and to Mr. Webster, having your name in the paper was a crime in itself. And he hadn't yet forgotten the ghastly night when one of the Irregulars' investigations had resulted in a police car coming to the door and Jeff being hauled off to the station suspected of theft. Of course it had all been cleared up, but the whole thing had left scars on Mr. Webster's conventional soul.

But on the other hand—Mr. Webster had great faith in his son's capabilities. He'd stood by him then, and he'd stand by him now. Drawing a deep breath, Mr. Webster picked up the phone. "Get me Mr. Carabosse, would you?" There was a longish pause, and then he said, "Mr. Carabosse? This is Mr. Webster, from the bank. It's about your robbery—still no news? Then in that case I think my son may be able to help you."

A quarter of an hour later, Jeff was standing in the luxuri-

ous office above the equally luxurious premises of Carabosse and Co., the biggest and poshest jewelers on High
Street. Properly speaking, it was *Carabosse et Cie*, since both
family and firm were French in origin. M. Carabosse had
lived in England for many years now, but still retained the
general manner, accent, and appearance of a typical
Frenchman. No doubt it went down well with the lady
customers. His two sons, Charles and André, had grown up
and gone to school in England and were completely an-
glicized. The really foreign one of the lot was Cousin Bruno,
a representative of the Paris branch of the family, over here
to improve his English.

Liz should have come on this job, thought Jeff sourly.
Maybe she'd enjoy being surrounded by tall, dark, and
handsome Frenchmen. The presence of so much Continen-
tal charm made Jeff feel uncomfortably short and Anglo-
Saxon. There was enough of his father in him to make him
feel that all foreigners were basically unpredictable. It
wasn't helped by the fact that all three young men were
chattering to each other in machine-gun French and laughing occasionally—at him, Jeff suspected darkly.

M. Carabosse clapped his hands, and there was instant
silence. M. Carabosse himself had treated Jeff with grave
politeness, though he was obviously puzzled by the request
from the bank. Perhaps he had decided that handing criminal investigation over to school kids was just another man-
ifestation of the eccentricity of the English.

With a dramatic gesture, M. Carabosse pointed to the
enormous safe that dominated the rear wall of the luxurious
office. *"Voilà!"*

Even Jeff's shaky French could cope with that. "I see what you mean. It does look pretty formidable."

"It is impregnable," said M. Carabosse simply. "Permit me!" He took a manufacturer's leaflet from the top of the safe and handed it to Jeff.

Rapidly Jeff read through it. The safe was the latest and most expensive model from a famous firm of locksmiths. It was guaranteed immune to any kind of attack, including explosives and the blow torch. It had a time lock, so that even with the right keys it could only be opened at pre-determined hours. And finally, if any attempt was made to tamper with it, it set off a variety of alarms, both in the shop and down at the nearby police station.

Jeff handed the leaflet back. "I see what you mean. And since no alarms were set off, it seems pretty clear no one even tried to crack it. Maybe you'd be good enough to tell me what happened. When did you discover the jewels were stolen?"

M. Carabosse pointed to the safe. "As you see, the safe is now closed. There are three keys. I have one—my sons André and Charles have the others." He produced an intricate-looking key from a chain in his pocket, and at a nod from their father, the two young men did the same.

M. Carabosse went on. "The safe is set to open at eight thirty each morning. At that time, we take the jewels from the safe, and place them in the display cabinets down-stairs—which are also protected by alarms, I might add. We close at six o'clock. At six fifteen the safe is reopened and the jewels placed inside. The safe is then closed until eight thirty the following morning."

"What happened the day the diamonds disappeared?"

M. Carabosse spread his hands. "Nothing! The jewels were placed in the safe the previous evening. Next morning, we opened the safe, the jewel cases were taken out and opened one by one—and the case that had held the necklace was empty."

"You *saw* the cases opened—here in this office? There was no chance anything was taken?"

"I will ignore the fact that the suggestion insults my family," said M. Carabosse coldly. "I *saw* Bruno take the case from the safe. I *saw* him open it. And I *saw* with my own eyes that it was empty. We all saw, did we not?"

There was a murmur of agreement from the three young men. Jeff scratched his head. "You're sure it was Bruno who opened that particular case? Does he remember it?" There was a quick rattle of French from the two brothers, and then Bruno said, "*I* open the case. The case is new, and the lock sticks for a moment." He had what Jeff couldn't help thinking of as an Inspector Clouseau accent.

"There is no chance that the jewels fell out—or something?" said Jeff lamely. In languid upper-class accents, André, the eldest son, said, "The necklace is worth over twenty thousand pounds. Do you really think we didn't look?"

M. Carabosse said, "Nothing fell out of the case, because the case was empty when it was opened. There is no possible doubt of it."

"So you called the police?"

"There was no alternative. Given the particular circumstances, I might have preferred not to, but one of our

English directors happened to be in the office when the safe was opened. He called the police."

"What happened when they arrived?"

Charles, the second son, said, "Not a lot! They didn't come for a couple of hours. Then a young bloke called Day arrived with a squad of so-called experts. They examined the safe and the jewel boxes inside, asked about a million questions, searched all of us and all our rooms, and then went off without finding a thing. I reckon they think it's a devious insurance fraud. Can't trust the French, you know!"

Jeff sighed, and looked around the office. There was a door beside the safe, and for no particular reason he asked, "What's in there?"

M. Carabosse opened the door, revealing rows of shelves lined with boxes and jewel cases. "It is a storeroom. The cases are empty. The police searched there too. They found nothing."

Jeff sighed, wishing desperately that he'd picked the truck hijackings or the missing man. Just his luck—he'd been landed with a genuine, copper-bottomed, impossible crime.

"Now if you will excuse me," said M. Carabosse politely, "I must return to the shop. My sons and their cousin will be happy to give you any more information you need."

He went down the stairs and Jeff was left facing the three young men. He felt they were all looking at him with supercilious scorn. André was tall and elegant, a younger version of his father. Charles was the most likable of them, but even he had a mocking grin on his face. And Bruno, the cousin, looked bored and resentful of the whole thing. They were all several inches taller than Jeff, and for some reason that seemed to make things harder.

Doggedly he took them through the crime again. Yes, exactly the same routine had been followed as on every other morning.

No, they had noticed nothing and no one unusual in the days preceding the crime.

Yes, they had all been extensively questioned by the police, a certain Detective-Sergeant Day, and at their own request they had all been searched. The entire shop had been thoroughly searched, come to that, and so had M. Carabosse's house, not far away, where they all lived.

The three young men stood together in a tight little group, and Jeff couldn't help feeling that they were ganging up against him, both as a foreigner and as someone who wasn't part of the family.

Bruno was the least cooperative of all, alternately giggling and sulking, and pretending not to be able to understand Jeff's English. Jeff made a halting attempt to question him in French, but languages had never been his strong point, and his attempts to speak French reduced Bruno and the others to helpless giggles.

Jeff looked suspiciously at the three young men. Maybe they were all in it, planning to split the proceeds. He felt sure of one thing. He wasn't going to solve this one, not on his own. Dan Robinson could take over this case, and welcome. Jeff asked a few more questions, then gave up. Just as he was leaving the shop, he bumped into Fred Summers. . . .

6 THE MAN WHO VANISHED

The elegant lady on the doorstep of the even more elegant house looked at Liz with disfavor. "No, I'm sorry, you can't see my husband. He's—away. Away on business."

Liz produced her most winning smile. "Then perhaps you could help me. It's a project for my school magazine, you see."

"A project? What about?"

Liz looked at the expensively carpeted hall and had a sudden inspiration. "On home decorating, actually. I was told that yours is one of the finest homes in the area, and I wondered if—"

The woman was obviously flattered. "Well, perhaps just a few minutes . . ."

She ushered Liz inside.

They spent most of the next hour touring the big house from top to bottom. The place was carpeted, draped, decorated, and furnished until you could scarcely move. Everything looked brand new and unused, and the whole place seemed completely unlived in, like a set display of rooms in a shop window. And it was all done in the most expensive and elaborate bad taste. The end of the tour was the pièce de résistance—the sunken bathtub with gold taps in the shape of dolphins. "Well, what do you think of *that*?"

"I've never seen anything like it," said Liz sincerely. "Tell me, Mrs. Fillmore, did you do all this yourself, or did your husband help you?"

Mrs. Fillmore gave a shriek of laughter. "James? All he's interested in is that old business of his. No, this is all my own work. Decor is so important, don't you agree?"

"Oh, yes," said Liz earnestly. She herself lived with her mum in a tiny top floor flat furnished from local junk shops. "Have we seen everything now? What about your husband's room? Isn't there a study, or anything like that?"

"Well, he's got a sort of office, downstairs next to the kitchen, but it's really not—"

"Must have the full picture, mustn't we," said Liz brightly, and before Mrs. Fillmore could stop her, she had slipped out of the bathroom and run down to the office.

Mr. Fillmore's office wasn't much bigger than a broom closet and it was furnished in a very similar style.

It held a wooden table, a wooden chair, and an old armchair with the stuffing coming out. The walls were decorated with building-trade catalogs and gardening calendars and amateur theater posters, and the desk held a pipe rack holding a couple of much used pipes.

Mrs. Fillmore gave a little trill of laughter. "Disgraceful, isn't it? Just like a garden shed. Still, that's how he likes it. I offered to have it redecorated, but he refused to let me change a thing." She edged Liz away and closed the office door.

"Have you any idea how long your husband will be away?" asked Liz.

Mrs. Fillmore sighed and suddenly became much more serious. "No, I haven't," she said. "I only wish I had." To her distress, Liz saw her eyes were filling with tears.

Mrs. Fillmore led her back into the immaculately gleaming kitchen, which seemed to have every household appliance ever invented. It was all a bit pointless, thought Liz, since presumably Mrs. Fillmore was now using it to cook meals for one—that is, if she did her own cooking at all.

"Would you like some coffee?" asked Mrs. Fillmore unexpectedly.

When Liz said yes, she made a great business of grinding fresh beans in an electric grinder and making the coffee in some complicated French device that had a sort of plunger on it—rather like those things they use for blowing up dynamite in Westerns.

Mrs. Fillmore wrestled with this apparatus and produced two cups of thick black coffee, ferociously strong. Liz sipped hers politely.

"I can't help worrying, you see," said Mrs. Fillmore suddenly. "I didn't at first. Once the children grew up and went away, he got very busy, and of course I had the house to see to. We both seemed to lead separate lives. But he was always there if I needed him, and he was very considerate. It isn't like him to just go off and not tell anyone. I actually went around to the police, you know."

"What happened?"

"Well, they sent someone around to see me. A rather impertinent young man called Day. He said there was nothing unusual about people disappearing; it happened all the time. He said people just get fed up with their everyday lives and wander off. Sometimes they come back, sometimes they don't. . . ."

"Maybe it's that," said Liz gently. "Don't worry, Mrs. Fillmore, I'm sure he's all right. He'll probably turn up again before too long."

"Yes," said Mrs. Fillmore brightly. "Yes, of course he will. Now, if you'll excuse me, I have a great deal to do."

It was clear that she was regretting having talked so much about her troubles to a perfect stranger. Liz thanked her politely and took her leave.

Half an hour later, she was parking her bicycle outside Fillmore and Patterson Limited. The firm's premises were at the end of a quiet tree-lined street and consisted of a big paved yard littered with fountains, gnomes, and garden furniture, with a scattered collection of warehouses, greenhouses, and garden sheds laid out behind it. It was a busy place. Cars were driving in and out all the time, and keen gardeners were everywhere, buying tools, sacks of fertilizer, benches, stone fountains, sundials, and all the other things keen gardeners seem to need. There was a prefabricated building in the center of the yard, which seemed to serve as a combination shop, warehouse, and office.

Inside it a couple of young men in overalls were serving the customers. Liz waited while a fat lady bought a particularly repulsive garden gnome, then collared the assistant, a skinny red-haired youth. "Excuse me, I'm looking for Mr. Fillmore."

"Away," said the youth briefly, and turned to a very small man with a large sack of fertilizer.

"Can you tell me when he'll be back?"

"No idea. Try the manager."

He nodded to a door in the corner of the room.

Liz went over to the door, tapped, and entered, without waiting for a reply. She found herself in a tiny cluttered office. Behind the desk a tall, thin, bespectacled man was on the telephone. "You tell your boss that I *must* have immediate cash payment— Hold on a moment." He put his hand over the mouthpiece of the phone. "What can I do for you?"

"I was looking for Mr. Fillmore."

"Why?"

"I want to interview him for our school magazine. We're doing a feature on local businessmen."

"Well, I'm afraid he's away. Anyway, I doubt if he'd talk to you, he hates any kind of publicity."

"Do you know when he'll be back?"

"No idea. Now, if you'll excuse me?"

He looked expectantly at Liz, and she had no alternative but to back out of the office, closing the door behind her. She heard the man's voice again. "I'm sorry, but shares will not be acceptable, the full payment must be made in cash."

Liz looked around the shop. All the assistants were busy, with lots of customers waiting to be served. She went out into the yard and looked around, wondering where to start her inquiries.

A voice behind her said, "Arternoon!" and Liz turned to see someone who seemed to have all the time in the world— a tubby, white-whiskered old man sat in a wheelbarrow in the doorway of a little wooden hut just beside the office. He wore ancient boots, even more ancient trousers, and what looked like about half a dozen assorted pullovers. A battered old hat in the general shape of a flowerpot was clamped on his head, and he was puffing peacefully on an old clay pipe.

"Good afternoon," said Liz a little uncertainly. "I was looking for Mr. Fillmore."

The old man chuckled. "So are they all, missy, so are they all! But who's to find him?"

"You know he's missing then?"

"Of course I do. Can't hide things from me, can they?"

He seemed a friendly, gossipy old man, and Liz decided he might be a useful source of information. "Do you know Mr. Fillmore well?"

"Know him? Know Jim Fillmore? I'd like to see the man that knows him better." He beckoned her closer. "I was with him in the war, see. Went through shot and shell together, we did. Then afterward we goes our separate ways. Jim Fillmore goes into this gardening lark and does well for himself."

"And what did you do?"

"Well, I could never settle, that was my trouble. Bit of this and a bit of that. Tell you the truth, I was pretty much on the tramp when I run into Jim again." The old man paused dramatically. "And does he scorn his old comrade in arms? Does he even slip me a fiver to be on me way? He does not!

Sam, he says, there's a billet here for life for you. Watchman and general handyman. Gets this little hut put up, and here I am. Take a look at this, eh?"

Liz peered inside the hut. Basically it was a wooden garden shed, but it had been furnished as a kind of cabin, with a bunk bed, an old wooden table, a couple of chairs, and a wheelbarrow fixed up as an armchair. There were sacking curtains at the windows, and even a little corner kitchen, with a small electric stove and an assortment of tin cups and plates. "You certainly seem very comfortable here."

"Comfortable. 'Tis a palace!" Suddenly Sam's face changed. "Now maybe you'll tell me why you're so interested in me old pal Jim?"

Liz hesitated, then said, "Because I'm trying to find out what's happened to him." Quickly she told him about the Baker Street Irregulars, leaving out Day's disappearance.

Sam listened in fascination. He lowered his voice. "Well, you've come to the right place, missy. There's things going on here, and I'm the one that can tell you about them."

"What kind of things?"

He jerked his head toward the office. "You see that tall skinny bloke with the glasses?"

"Mr. Patterson? Mr. Fillmore's partner? I had a word with him just now. He said Mr. Fillmore was away on holiday. He was too busy to talk for long."

Sam sniffed. "Busy. I'll say he's busy. Trips up to big bankers in the city, meetings with blokes who turn up in big limousines. It's a big job, selling a company the size of this."

"Selling? You mean Mr. Patterson's selling the business? While his partner's away?"

"That's right."

"But he wouldn't be able to. I mean, Mr. Fillmore would have to sign papers and things."

"There's ways of making people sign papers. Or there's forgeries," said Sam darkly.

Liz looked at him in astonishment. "You really think he's done something to Mr. Fillmore—and now he's selling the business?"

"Ssssh!" said the old man suddenly. "He's seen us."

Liz looked up and saw Patterson crossing the yard. He strode over to the hut and stood glaring down at them. "What's going on here? Haven't you got any work to do, Sam?"

The old man heaved himself out of his wheelbarrow armchair. "Just finishing me tea break, Mr. Patterson. Man has to have a break." With a conspiratorial wink at Liz, he took a big birch broom from behind the door of the hut and began sweeping his way slowly across the yard.

"Silly old fool," muttered Patterson. "What's he been telling you?"

"Oh, nothing," said Liz hurriedly. "Just chatting about Mr. Fillmore, and what good friends they were."

"You're sure that was all?"

Liz decided to probe for a reaction. "Well, he did seem worried about Mr. Fillmore. He was sort of hinting there might be something wrong."

She got her reaction, but it wasn't quite the one she expected. Patterson looked at the old man with a kind of sardonic amusement in his eyes. "Oh, did he? Then let me tell you this, young lady: If anyone knows what's happened to Jim Fillmore, it's old Sam."

"What makes you say that?"

Like Sam before him, Patterson lowered his voice confi-
dentially. "Let me put it this way. This old tramp turns up
out of nowhere, claims to be Jim's long-lost friend. Well, Jim
doesn't seem any too pleased to see him. They go off for a
long chat, and before you know where you are, Jim takes
him on as watchman, gives him free accommodation, and
pays him a salary about ten times what he's worth." He
glanced across at the old man, who was doing his slow-
motion sweeping on the other side of the yard, obviously
well aware that he was being talked about. "Mind you, any
salary would be more than he's worth, since he never does a
stroke of work anyway. Yet Jim wouldn't hear a word
against him. And the funny thing is, I could swear he can't
stand the fellow."

"Are you saying they weren't such great friends after all?"

"You never saw them together," said Mr. Patterson simply. Again he gave her a look of sardonic amusement.

"Then why would Mr. Fillmore be so nice to him—if he
didn't actually like him."

"Maybe he didn't have any choice."

"Blackmail?"

Mr. Patterson shrugged. "Who knows? But I'll tell you
something else, since you're so curious. Old Sam was the last
person to set eyes on him."

"What happened?"

"It was late one evening. Jim had been moody all day.
When we'd closed up, he said he'd stay on for a bit. Said he
wanted to talk to old Sam. He was muttering something
about having it out with him and not standing for any
more." Mr. Patterson lowered his voice dramatically. "As I

drove away, I saw him walking into old Sam's hut. I never saw him again. He didn't turn up next day, and no one's seen him since."

"Have you searched the yard?"

"Well, we had a look around, but there was no trace of him. But—"

"But what?"

"There's a couple of acres of flower beds and seed beds behind here. And old Sam does a lot of digging!"

"Didn't you tell the police?"

"Jim's wife reported him missing eventually. The police sent some lad of a detective-sergeant around here, but he didn't seem very concerned. Said people disappear all the time, just get fed up and wander off, it isn't a crime. . . ." Mr. Patterson straightened up. "Well, can't stay here chatting to you, I've got work to do. But I thought I'd better warn you. I wouldn't spend too much time hanging around old Sam. It might not be safe!"

Patterson went back toward his office, leaving Liz staring after him.

Suddenly a voice whispered in her ear. "How about coming back to my hut, missy, for a nice cuppa tea? We could go on with our chat about poor old Jim."

Old Sam had crept silently up behind her.

Liz jumped about a foot in the air and whirled around. "No, I'm afraid I've got to be on my way. Maybe I'll come back another time."

She ran to her bike, unlocked it, and pedaled furiously into the distance.

Old Sam stood looking after her, a curious smile on his

whiskered lips. Then he turned and went back into his hut. Settling himself in his wheelbarrow, he relit his clay pipe and was soon puffing peacefully away.

After a moment Patterson came out of the office and across to him. "Been letting your tongue run away with you, Sam?"

Sam chuckled. "Wanted to play detective, didn't she? I was just giving her a bit to think about." Briefly Sam recounted what Liz had told him about the Baker Street Irregulars.

"Those kids are supposed to be pretty bright, you know," said Patterson. "Suppose she gets on to the truth?"

"What does it matter? The deal's nearly through, isn't it?"

Patterson nodded. "They just confirmed over the phone. I had to take a slightly lower price to get immediate cash."

Old Sam cackled evilly. "There you are then! As soon as we get our hands on that money, those nosy kids can ask all the questions they like. They'll never find Jim Fillmore— and neither will anyone else!"

7 THE BEAR

Micky feinted, slipped past the opposing defender, and shot. The goalkeeper leaped, missed, and the ball thudded against the fence, just inside the chalked goalpost.

There was a roar from the crowd—which in this case consisted of a handful of older men sitting around drinking tea from their Thermos flasks.

Mickey had spent the afternoon hanging around Anderson Transport, and now he was guest center forward in a scratch soccer game organized by the young apprentices during their tea break.

He'd found the men a friendly, chatty crowd and had given the impression that he was Anderson's nephew paying an unexpected visit. Only Burton, the big security man, still seemed suspicious of him. He seemed to be all over the place, trying doors and gates, checking the fences, inspecting the trucks as they came in and out. The men didn't care much for him either, laughing and making fun of him behind his back, and obviously thinking him a fool for his excessive zeal. Even Mr. Sowery, the foreman, seemed to agree with them. "Nowt wrong wi' a fair day's work for a fair day's pay, lad," he said to Mickey. "I do that meself, and I make sure everyone else does. But that chap fair knocks himself out. He never stops; you'd think he owned the place."

Mickey had enjoyed this afternoon, but he'd found nothing suspicious, no clues as to who might be behind the hijackings. Mr. Anderson seemed both popular and respected. The men said he was a good boss. "Even turns a blind eye to your moonlighting, doesn't he, Jacko?" said Sowery.

Jacko, a wizened little man in a cloth cap, grinned sheepishly. "Leave it alone, Fred."

"What's moonlighting?" asked Mickey innocently.

"Well, Jacko here does one or two private repair jobs, you see. Cars, radios, TV, stuff like that. On his own time, like, but using the firm's premises and equipment. One night Mr. Anderson's here late too, and he comes in and catches Jacko working on a crunched-up mini. Doesn't say a word. Next day, he sends for Jacko and says, 'I'm having a bit of trouble with my gearbox, Jacko. Take a look at it, will you? I'll leave it here tonight.' So Jacko fixes the gearbox, and next morning he ups and asks the boss for fifteen quid." Sowery laughed. "You know what the boss said?"

"What?"

" 'Fifteen quid nothing,' he says. 'While you're getting free use of my premises and my tools, I'm getting free car repairs,' he says. And he does. Old Jacko's been doing all his car repairs free ever since!"

There was an appreciative chuckle from the little group. Obviously the story was a familiar one and had been told many times.

Sowery looked at his watch. "Tea break's over, lads. Back on the job."

The little group scattered and Mickey resumed his wandering around. He might just as well give up and go home, he decided. Or better still, he'd go around and report to Dan Robinson. Maybe Dan could work out what was going on.

Before he went home, Mickey decided to take a last look at the American Bear. He slipped out of the workshop, crossed to the annex where the big machine was housed, and stood staring in fascination at the huge truck held fast in the spider's web of steel.

Suddenly a thought struck him. This truck was one of the ones that had been hijacked . . . only the hijack had gone wrong. Mickey had already decided that someone was marking the trucks that carried valuable cargo so that the thieves could pick them out. Suppose that marking device, whatever it was, was still in or on the truck?

Mickey walked all around the machine, studying the truck from every angle. There seemed nothing to be seen on the outside of the machine. . . . Mickey stood thinking hard. Maybe it wasn't a visual signal at all. Maybe some kind of calling device—and the natural place for that would be underneath the truck.

Mickey took a deep breath. The chassis was suspended a few feet above the ground, and there was plenty of room for him. Lying flat on his back, he slithered under the cab. Reaching up, he began feeling over the underside of the

cab. It was coated with dirt and grease, and he soon realized
that the task was hopeless. The thing to do, Mickey decided,
was to go and tell Mr. Anderson of his theory and get him to
organize a proper search.

He was about to wriggle out when he heard the annex
door open. He saw booted feet and overalled legs crossing
the concrete floor to the control panel.

"Hey, hang on a minute," yelled Mickey, and started to
wriggle out. He was too late. There was a low groaning
sound, a sudden shriek of tortured metal, and the truck
chassis slipped from its fastenings and dropped on top of
him.

The overalled figure went out of the annex, closing the
door behind him.

Dan Robinson lay stretched out on his bed, reading and
rereading Day's notebook. He put the notebook aside, letting his mind wander. Which of the three criminals had
been so terrified of detection that they had framed and
kidnapped a detective-sergeant of police? The jewel thief
who'd gotten away with an impossible crime? The somebody or somebodies who'd caused the disappearance of an
inconspicuous supplier of gardening requisites? Or the
gang of professional criminals behind the truck hijackings?
Like Mickey, Dan favored the third possibility.

But the others had to be checked out. The trouble was, he
couldn't be in three places at once, and following up any one
lead meant neglecting the other two.

That was why it had seemed such a good idea to send out
his three Irregulars, one to each crime. Once they'd re-

ported back, he'd know which case to concentrate on. The trouble was, it left him nothing to do meanwhile.

Dan looked at his watch. It was past teatime. Where were they all? He'd told them to have a quick scout around and report back. No doubt they were trying to solve the cases on their own. Especially young Mickey . . .

Dan got up, picking up the notebook for a last look at it. There was a fourth possibility, of course. That scrawled car number on the last page, the name Domingues, and the note about failing to stop for a zebra crossing. Dan grinned. Maybe that was the one! Some fanatically keen motorist so proud of his spotless record that he'd kidnap a copper rather than have it marred by a careless driving charge. It didn't seem very likely.

Tossing the book on his desk, Dan went downstairs.

He was just pouring boiling water into the teapot when Jeff mooched into the kitchen, muttered "Hello, Dan," and slumped into a chair.

Dan looked at him. "Well, I can see you've come rushing around with a load of vital information. You look fed up to the teeth."

"So would you be, if you'd spent the afternoon being sneered at by a load of Frenchmen."

"Now, now, don't let's be chauvinist," said Dan reprovingly. "Let me cheer you up with a decent British cup of tea and some guaranteed British rock cakes."

Over tea Jeff gave an explosive account of his afternoon. "Somehow or other they manage to give you the impression you ought to be living in a cave and painting yourself blue with woad. The father acts as if he thought he was Louis the

Fourteenth, and André the eldest son's not much better. Charles, the second son, is quite human, but as for Cousin Bruno . . . To cap it all, I met Summers on the steps, and he gave me a good telling off."

Eventually Jeff calmed down enough to give an account of his investigation and of the seemingly impossible way in which the necklace had disappeared. "I reckon it must be an inside job," he concluded. "The shop and the safe are stiff with alarms, and none of them were set off. So it must have been one of the family. Maybe it's some kind of insurance swindle, and they're all in it." He looked at Dan. "Well, what do you make of it?"

Dan took him over the whole thing again, drawing out everything Jeff had seen, and everything everyone else had said and done. Jeff had spent most of the afternoon at the shop, poking around and trying to question people, but he got the idea that no one was taking him seriously. "That Cousin Bruno was the worst," he said darkly. "All he'd do was gabble French, giggle, and do silly conjuring tricks. Have you ever tried to interrogate someone who keeps on taking fifty-pence pieces out of your ear?" He looked at Dan. "Well, what do you make of it?"

Dan put his finger tips together. "The case does present one or two interesting features," he said teasingly. "However, I don't think the problem should be too difficult to solve."

Jeff looked hard at him, wondering if he was bluffing. Before he could demand explanations, Liz burst into the room.

If Jeff's entrance had been low-key, Liz's more than made

up for it in drama. "Dan, you've got to come at once. I'm sure he got rid of that poor man, and he looked quite capable of getting rid of poor Day as well. We've got to tell the police."

Dan managed to calm her down, poured her tea, and finally managed to get a reasonably coherent account of her two visits, first to Mrs. Fillmore, and then to the gardening-supplies warehouse. When she finished her account of her encounters with Mr. Patterson and Old Sam, Dan said, "It certainly looks as if something pretty sinister's going on, doesn't it? If you've had too little success, Jeff, Liz seems to have had almost too much!"

"The stories contradict each other," objected Jeff. "Did Patterson get rid of his partner so he could sell the business? Or is Old Sam a blackmailer who disposed of his victim when he wouldn't pay up anymore?"

"There is a third possibility," said Liz. "Suppose they're both in it together, Old Sam and Patterson, and they told me two different stories just to confuse the investigation? Both stories sound pretty phony, now I've had time to think."

"That's not a bad idea, Liz," said Dan approvingly. "And I think you're partly right."

"Only partly?"

Dan smiled infuriatingly. "There is a fourth possibility, one that neither of you seems to have thought of—"

Once again he was interrupted, this time by the telephone. Dan listened for a moment, and then said, "No, he's not here, Mrs. Denning, but I think I know where he is. Don't worry, we'll go and find him and pack him off home." He put down the phone and turned to the others. "Mickey's mum. He's not back for his tea, and she wondered if he's with us." Dan looked at Liz and Jeff. "Mickey went off first, and he's been gone the longest—and we gave him the most promising lead. What's the betting he stumbled on something suspicious, tried to investigate it himself, and landed up in trouble?"

"Knowing Mickey, about ten to one in favor," said Liz.

"More like a hundred to one," said Jeff.

Dan stood up. "Come on, we'd better go and sort the little perisher out."

It was only because Mickey was a little perisher, small and skinny, that he was still alive. The truck chassis had crashed to the floor at an angle, and the two side girders were poised about six inches from the concrete floor. In those few inches there was—just—enough room for Mickey. He wasn't injured, he wasn't even hurt, but he was completely and utterly trapped, with the girder exactly across his middle.

He tried to wriggle forward, but it was clear that his head wouldn't go under the girder. He tried to wriggle back, but the edge of the metal caught on his hip bone. There was no way out. Worse still, as he struggled, the metal beam groaned and seemed to settle on him more firmly. Mickey stopped struggling. He sensed that the beam was delicately poised, and if he didn't want to end up in two separate halves . . .

From somewhere outside he heard a whistle, followed by footsteps, distant voices, the sound of hurrying feet, cars starting up and driving away. It must be half past five. Mr. Anderson's men were going home.

Mickey started to feel the beginnings of panic. At the very least he would have to stay here all night, until someone came to check on the machine. And if the wrecked chassis settled further ...

Somehow he *had* to get free.

He looked around, seeing if there was anything within reach that might help him. A scattering of objects had fallen around him, presumably shaken from the truck when it fell. There was a wrench, a few bits of oily rag, some oddly shaped bits of metal. Nothing useful, like a blow torch or even a file. He reached for the wrench and found that he could just touch it with his fingers. As he edged it toward him, a curious thing happened. A circular piece of metal lying close to the wrench started to move as well. Suddenly Mickey realized why. It was magnetic, attracted by the wrench. Soon both wrench and disk were in easy reach.

Mickey picked up the disk and squinted at it. It was smooth and round like a tiny flying saucer. Maybe it was a clue. He stuck it in his shirt pocket and turned his attention to escape. All he had was the wrench. That, a piece of oil-soaked rag in reach of his other hand, and the concrete floor ...

Mickey lifted the wrench and slammed it down as hard as he could on the floor. To his delight, there was a spark ... quite a big one.

He edged the oil-soaked rag closer to the wrench. He began smashing the spanner rhythmically against the concrete floor. . . .

Mr. Anderson was sitting in his office working on a complicated-looking list when Dan, Liz, and Jeff burst into the room, with the security man and his dog close on their heels. Rather than stopping to explain, they'd cycled straight up to the main office.

After a certain amount of confusion, Mr. Anderson gathered who they were, and listened while Dan explained their anxiety about Mickey.

"He was here all right," he said. "Nice little kid, full of beans. I hired him to solve the case as sort of a joke. When there was no sign of him at closing time, I assumed he'd got fed up and gone home with the lads. You have any idea where he is, Burton?"

The security man shook his head. "I thought I saw him going off with the lads, but I can't be sure. It's such a stampede when that siren goes. . . ."

Mr. Anderson put the list he was working on into a folder and locked the folder away in the old-fashioned safe in the corner. "We'd best go and look for him. Mind you, he could take some finding. This is a big place, and it's full of nooks and crannies."

Suddenly he cocked his head. "Listen!" From somewhere outside there came the clangor of a fire alarm.

Mr. Anderson rushed out of his office and into the yard, the others close behind him. He stood poised, listening, then said, "It's coming from the annex!" He set off across the yard at a run.

When they opened the annex door, an extraordinary sight met their eyes. The truck chassis lay on its side in the middle of the big room. Close beside it was a smoldering pile of oily rags. The smoke from the rags had triggered the smoke-detector system, set off the alarms, and activated the sprinkler system, so that a light summer rain seemed to be falling in the room. A pair of jeaned legs ending in shabby sneakers were projecting from underneath a massive girder poised inches above the floor.

As they stood staring in horror, Mickey's indignant voice came from somewhere under the chassis. "Don't just stand there gawking—get me out!"

8 THE TRAP

Jeff ran forward to pull Mickey free, but Mr. Anderson held him back. "Hang on, that whole thing's finely balanced. Start heaving about and the whole lot could come down on him."

It was Jeff who saw the solution. "We need jacks, big ones!"

"Storeroom," said Mr. Anderson instantly. "Come on!"

Liz stayed with Mickey, while Dan, Jeff, and Burton ran off after Mr. Anderson. "Don't move, Mickey," she called. "Don't even breathe. We'll soon get you out!"

"You'd better," came Mickey's voice. "If this thing comes down any further, I'll be *squeezed* out—like toothpaste!"

Liz shuddered.

Minutes later the others were back, staggering under the weight of the jacks. Under Anderson's guidance, they positioned them at intervals along the girder, winding the jacks up to support the beam.

When all four jacks refused to be wound further, Anderson paused, mopping his forehead. "That's stopped it coming down any further—but I don't think we've actually *raised* it much! Let's see if we can pull him free."

They grabbed Mickey's legs and pulled steadily. His body moved a few inches and then stuck. Mickey gave a yell of anguish and said bitterly that he'd like to come out in one piece if it was all the same to them, and preferably not a foot taller either.

"Oil!" said Liz suddenly. She spotted a can of heavy-duty machine oil in the corner, and ran to fetch it. Unscrewing the lid, she began pouring the heavy oil onto Mickey's middle at the point where he disappeared under the beam, ignoring his yells of protest. When Mickey was lying in the middle of a big puddle of oil, she turned to the others. "All right, heave!"

They heaved steadily—and suddenly Mickey shot out from under the girder, like a reluctant sardine leaving its tin.

Ten minutes later they were all sitting in Mr. Anderson's office drinking sweet tea—all except Burton, who had been sent back on guard. Liz was on the phone to Mickey's mother. "Yes, honestly, Mrs. Denning, he's fine." She crossed her fingers. "The thing is he's a bit wet, he fell into a canal. If I could just pop around and pick up some clothes for him, we'll let you have him back all washed and dried. No, honestly, it's no trouble." It took a bit more talking, but Mrs. Denning agreed at last, and Liz put down the phone with a sigh of relief.

"Well done, Liz," said Jeff. "If ever a job needed a woman's touch ..."

"Coward," said Liz scornfully. "Still, we can't send him home like this, can we? His mum would murder him."

"And us," said Jeff.

Mickey's mum, like his dad and his brothers, was large and formidable.

Mickey was an extraordinary sight, soaking wet, covered with oil, dirt, and grime. But nevertheless he was quite undaunted and was busily giving Dan a full account of his discoveries and adventures, including the fact that someone had deliberately dropped the truck chassis on him—and showing the magnetic round disk he'd found.

Mr. Anderson shook his head despairingly. "This is all my fault," he said. "I should have known a gang of kids couldn't solve anything like this."

"On the contrary," said Dan. "We've already solved it. If you'd like to go along with us, we can wrap it up for you. But we'll need a bit more cooperation."

Mr. Anderson looked dazedly at him. "Like what?"

"I take it those were the duty rosters you were typing up—the list that tells you what truck's carrying what?"

Mr. Anderson nodded.

"We'd better make it easy for them," said Dan thoughtfully. "Have you got any security vans?"

Mr. Anderson led him into the secretary's office, which looked out onto the truck parking lot. "You see that blue van over there?"

"The one with Chang's Chinese Laundry on it?"

"That's right. A fully protected security van—disguised, see?"

"Couldn't be better," said Dan happily. "Now then, I want

you to type a very special item in the duty roster for—let's say, day after tomorrow. The police will need a bit of time to get set up. Then I'll need you to come around to the police station with me. We've got a very skeptical detective-sergeant to convince."

Later that evening the Irregulars converged on Dan's house and found him frying a late-night supper of bacon and eggs in the kitchen. His parents had gone out for the evening, and as usual, Dan and Baskerville were alone in the big old house.

Dan waved the skillet at them. "Anyone for bacon and eggs? I can soon fry up some more."

"No, thanks, we've had supper," said Liz. "What we want from you is not eggs, but explanations."

"That's right," said Mickey, who was now bathed, changed and very much himself again. "Why did you pack us all off home? And what have you been fixing up with Anderson?"

Dan scooped bacon and eggs onto a plate and sat down to eat. Baskerville sat hopefully at his elbow, hoping for bacon scraps.

"I'm afraid you'll have to wait for a bit," Dan said calmly. "So far I've only got theories. I won't be sure of the facts until the day after tomorrow."

There was a roar of protest, and Dan found himself with a near mutiny on his hands.

"It's just not fair," yelled Mickey. "I do all the work, I get squashed by trucks and boiled in oil. . . . You sit there calmly saying you've worked everything out—and you won't tell us."

"Don't worry, Mickey. You're not the only one," said Jeff bitterly. "*I* spent the afternoon getting sneered at by a load of supercilious Frenchmen, and he did the same thing to me."

"And me!" said Liz. "I only got scared out of my wits by a couple of homicidal gardeners. We get the hard work and the puzzles, and Sherlock Robinson sits there saying it's all clear as day!"

Dan mopped up his egg yolk with a bit of bread. "Well, it is," he said placidly. "Mind you, it's all theories at the moment, I need one or two facts to confirm them. But basically all three cases are already solved."

"Prove it," challenged Jeff. "What about my jewel robbery?"

Dan got up. "According to Day's notebook, M. Carabosse lives on Archdeacon's Avenue. It's only ten minutes away. We'll pop around and have a word with him."

Jeff stared at him. "Now?"

"Why not? It's a nice summer evening. The walk will do you good." He tossed Baskerville a scrap of bacon and made for the door.

A quarter of an hour later they were all standing outside an imposing mansion on Archdeacon's Avenue. This was the poshest street in the area, popularly known as Millionaire's Row. It was the kind of street where you were out of place if you didn't have a Rolls, and the driveways were littered with the family's second cars, humbler breeds like Porsches, Jaguars, and Ferraris.

M. Carabosse's mansion had a large and imposing pillared porch, and Liz, Jeff, and Mickey felt overawed. Dan, however, seemed quite unimpressed. He stepped forward and tugged the old-fashioned bellpull. A bell rung somewhere in the house. After a while the door opened. For a moment Jeff thought it was actually a butler, and then he recognized M. Carabosse, resplendent in evening dress.

He looked coldly at the little group. "Yes? What do you want?"

Jeff cleared his throat nervously. "I came to see you this morning."

M. Carabosse peered at him. "Ah, yes, the boy detective," he said. "I permitted you to waste my time this morning as a courtesy to your father, but enough is enough. My wife and I are entertaining guests. I will be very much obliged if you will go away immediately."

He was about to close the door when Dan stepped forward. *"Je suis navré de vous déranger à cette heure, Monsieur Carabosse, mais je crois que c'est bien possible que je peux vous donner un bon coup de main, non seulement en retrouvant les bijoux perdus. Il s'agit de l'honneur de votre famille."*

Mickey turned to Liz, who was standing beside him at the back of the group. "Crikey, what was all that about?"

"Something about finding the jewels and the family honor," whispered Liz.

Mickey looked at Dan in admiration. To him French was a kind of secret code that you wrestled with at school. It had never occurred to him that you could actually speak it—and as for addressing a foreigner in his own language . . .

M. Carabosse looked hard at Dan. *"Vous parlez serieusement, jeune homme?"*

"Bien sûr!"

"Entrez."

He waved them inside.

They followed him across a magnificent mirror-lined hall and into an even more splendid study, lined with the kind of leather-bound books that millionaires buy by the yard.

M. Carabosse sat down behind the desk and looked expectantly at Dan. *"Asseyez-vous."*

Dan sat down in the chair on the other side of the desk.

Liz, Jeff, and Mickey squeezed themselves onto a leather sofa at the end of the room.

To their annoyance, Dan went on talking French. *"D'abord, Monsieur Carabosse, je dois vous demander si vos fils et leur cousin sont chez vous ce soir?"*

"Non, je crois qu'ils sont allés au disco."

"Now what's he on about?" hissed Mickey.

"Dan was asking if the boys were at home, and he said no, they were at a disco."

Dan leaned forward. *"Alors, permettez-moi d'expliquer mes idées. . . ."*

The rest of the conversation was conducted in a rattle of low, urgent French, and Liz was unable to catch more than a few words. Dan spoke for some time. M. Carabosse listened, then he asked questions, and Dan answered them.

Dan spoke again, apparently suggesting some scheme. M. Carabosse listened, seemed to agree, stood up and shook hands with Dan, and suddenly the Irregulars were outside on the street again.

Dan turned to his friends and said mischievously, "There you are then. I hope you're all satisfied."

"Satisfied!" howled Mickey. "We get stuck there listening to you jabbering away in French and you ask if we're satisfied!"

"Come on, Liz," said Jeff. "Tell us what it was all about."

"Well, I missed quite a lot of it, but as far as I can gather, Dan wants us all to go to Carabosse's shop early tomorrow for a reconstruction of the crime. Is that right, Dan?"

"That's right. A quarter past eight sharp. Don't be late, or you'll miss all the fun."

"Quarter past eight—in holiday time?" protested Mickey. Not getting up in time for school was one of his greatest pleasures.

"Don't worry," said Dan. "I'll be there even earlier. . . ."

Next morning, bleary-eyed but prompt, Liz, Jeff, and Mickey assembled on the doorstep of Carabosse and Co.

They rang the bell, and M. Carabosse himself came to the door. Gravely he beckoned them to enter.

Upstairs in the office they found Dan. He was kneeling in the storeroom, surrounded by piles of empty jewel cases. There was a pair of old-fashioned kitchen scales in front of him—Liz remembered seeing them in Dan's mother's kitchen—and he seemed to have been weighing one jewel box against another. As they came into the room he straightened up, an empty jewel box in his hands. "Well done, you're just in time for the show." He handed the jewel box to M. Carabosse, came out of the storeroom, and closed the door behind him.

A few minutes later, three young Frenchmen came into the room. One was a younger version of M. Carabosse, the second was a pleasant, open-faced young man a couple of years younger than the first, and the third a sulkily handsome youth with a lock of hair falling over one eye.

They looked in astonishment at the four Irregulars. Gravely, M. Carabosse performed introductions. "Mademoiselle Spencer, Messieurs Webster, Denning, and Robinson—may I present my son André, my son Charles, and their Cousin Bruno." There were murmurs of *"Enchanté"* and handshakes all around.

Then M. Carabosse said, "Now, Monsieur Robinson has something to say to us."

Dan stepped forward and said—in English, to Mickey's vast relief, "We're going to reenact the moment when you discovered the loss of the jewels. First of all, we've got to open the safe, which should be possible just about—now."

The huge safe whirred and clicked. M. Carabosse produced his key, André and Charles produced theirs, and the safe door swung open.

Dan said, "Naturally the case that held the necklace is no longer in the safe, so we'll use an empty one from the storeroom as a substitute. M. Carabosse will put the case in the safe, reset the timer for eight thirty-five, and we'll carry out the reenactment."

M. Carabosse held out the open empty case, closed it, and put it into the safe. He adjusted a time clock set inside the door, closed the safe, stepped back, and waited.

It was a very long five minutes, but finally the safe whirred and clicked once again.

The ritual with the keys was repeated, and the safe door swung open.

M. Carabosse produced a list. "One diamond necklace." Nobody moved. "*Allez*, Bruno," he said sharply.

Moving as if hypnotized, Bruno stepped forward and took the case which M. Carabosse had just put into the safe.

"Open it," said Dan quietly.

Fumblingly, Bruno opened the jewel case. A diamond necklace lay blazing against the black velvet-lined interior of the case.

9 THE ACTOR

Bruno stared at the necklace in unbelieving fascination.

Dan stepped swiftly forward and took the case from his unresisting hands. "Of course, that isn't what you did on the morning of the robbery. In fact, you did the opposite—like this!" Dan closed the case, fumbled with the catch, opened it again, and held it out.

The case was empty.

Bruno whirled around and dashed from the room.

Instinctively Jeff started in pursuit, but M. Carabosse held him back. "No. Let him go."

Dan turned the jewel case upside down, fumbled with the catch, turned it right way up, opened it again—and there was the necklace. He passed the case to André. "Now you see it, now you don't. Simple, when you know how!"

"Mon brave jeune homme," said M. Carabosse emotionally. To Dan's utter horror—and the delight of the other three Irregulars—he stepped forward, enfolded Dan in a hug, and kissed him solemnly on both cheeks.

"That'll teach you to show off, Robbo," said Mickey later. They were eating a second breakfast in a café on High Street, and he was tucking into bacon, egg, French fries and beans, unlike the rest, who were content with coffee and rolls. "I didn't realize they did that in real life!"

It had taken them some time to get away from the jewelers. There had been quite an emotional scene, with hugs, handshakes, and congratulations, though, to Dan's relief, no more kisses. M. Carabosse had made several attempts to press money on Dan, and when he'd refused, much to Mickey's disgust, M. Carabosse had insisted on presenting Liz with a small diamond pin, which she felt sure was terrifyingly valuable.

Liz fingered the pin, which was gleaming in her lapel. "How did you know it was the jewel case, Dan?"

"Well, it had to be, didn't it?"

"But the police checked everything in the safe," objected Jeff. "Surely they checked the case as well?"

"They checked what was *in* the safe," said Dan. "That's where old Bruno was so clever. You can imagine, there was a right old hoo-ha when the necklace disappeared. People rushing about, checking the safe, searching the shop. . . . During all the fuss, he simply switched the trick case for one in the storeroom, so when the police came they checked an ordinary case—and found nothing. No one thought of checking all the *empty* cases in the storeroom—why should they?"

"No one except you," said Mickey admiringly. "How did you find the right one out of all those?"

"I weighed each empty case in the storeroom against an

ordinary one from the safe. The trick case was a bit heavier, partly because of the jewels, partly because of the mechanism inside. So when the scales went down I knew I'd found the right one."

"I can see why he put the case in the storeroom," said Jeff. "But why did he leave it there?"

"Where better? Like hiding a tree in a forest. The police searched everyone's rooms. Bruno's visit was due to end soon, and he reckoned on going home with the necklace in his pocket."

"I suppose it makes sense," said Jeff. "What puzzles me is, why did he steal the necklace in such a melodramatic way?"

"Why did he steal it at all, come to that?" asked Liz.

Dan finished his coffee. "One thing at a time. Start with the method. The one advantage about the so-called impossible crime is, it gets everyone thinking about the *how* and takes their mind off the *who*. Bruno knew he was bound to be suspected; he was the outsider, after all. So if he could steal the necklace in a way that looked as if *nobody* could have stolen it, then *anyone* could have stolen it. I think old Carabosse was secretly afraid one of his sons was involved. Bruno reckoned on him hushing the whole thing up for the sake of the family honor. They probably wouldn't even have involved the police if their English director hadn't been in the office." Dan turned to Liz. "As for why, the usual reason— money. Bruno left home under a bit of a cloud, apparently, a pile of debts and some very dubious friends. I imagine he saw a chance to score off his English relatives and make some easy money. Apparently this isn't the first time things have disappeared around Bruno."

"Where did he get the box from?" asked Mickey.

"Brought it with him, I imagine. It's a simple enough mechanism, a section of the bottom slides back when you press the catch in a certain way, and the necklace drops into a secret compartment. Once Jeff said Bruno liked doing conjuring tricks . . ."

"What'll happen to him?" asked Liz.

Dan grinned. "Apparently he's due to do his *service* any day now. The French still have national military service, you know. The family are hoping a spell in the army will make a man of him."

"A spell in the French Foreign Legion, that's what he needs," said Mickey. He drenched his last French fry with catsup and popped it in his mouth. "Right, what do we do now?" he said indistinctly.

Dan finished his coffee. "Nothing's going to happen about the hijackings till tomorrow. So why don't we just pop around and find Mr. Fillmore?"

It was still early when they parked their bikes outside Fillmore's Gardening Supplies, and the place was deserted. The door of Old Sam's hut stood open, but to Liz's relief there was no sign of him.

"That the homicidal maniac's lair?" asked Dan.

Liz nodded.

"Right," said Dan. "In we go! I need one or two facts to confirm my theories."

Somewhat nervously, Liz led the way, and the Irregulars crowded into the little hut.

Dan stood looking keenly around him—Sherlock

Holmes to the life, thought Liz. He pounced on the clay pipe, which lay in the tin-lid ashtray on the wooden table. There was some half-burned tobacco in the bowl of the pipe. Dan dug it out with a penknife and shredded the black and yellow flakes in the palm of his hand. "Well, I may not have written a monograph on cigar ash, like Sherlock Holmes, but I know an expensive Latakia mixture when I see one." He turned over the tin lid, revealing a black-and-white picture of two peasant women standing beside a line of loaded tobacco wagons. "There you are, Balkan Sobranie, not one of the cheapest brands on the market."

Dan examined the camp bed. "Here we have a bed with a sacking quilt—and good quality linen sheets."

"So he's got expensive tastes," said Liz. "He said himself he'd come down in the world."

Dan lifted some paperbacks down from a shelf. "Penguin plays, a book on Bertolt Brecht—oh, and a National Theatre Diary. Expensive and cultured tastes!" There was a wooden box on the shelf, and Dan took it down. It held several sticks of crayonlike substance in different shades. "Stage makeup—and look at this!" Dan held up a tattered fringe of white hair. "A false beard! Was Old Sam's beard false, Liz?"

Liz tried to summon up a picture of the old man. "No, it was real; I'd swear it was."

Mickey scratched his head. "So, why does a bloke with a real beard need a false one?"

"Why indeed?" said Dan softly. But he was smiling delightedly, as if each new discovery confirmed his theory—whatever it was.

"Come on, Dan," said Jeff. "Let's have it—what do you think's going on?"

"Well, it's all very simple really," began Dan—and a shadow fell over the little hut.

"Prying, are you?" said a voice.

Liz looked up and saw Old Sam standing in the doorway of the hut. His face was twisted into a terrifying scowl, and he held an enormous gleaming scythe in his hand. " 'Tis dangerous to be too curious. Poor Jim Fillmore was curious about Old Sam—and no one's seen him since."

The Irregulars were petrified with horror—but only for a moment. Liz gave a sweet smile and said, "Hello, Sam," wondering if she could charm him back into a good humor.

Mickey poised himself to spring—if he could dive between Sam's legs and bring him down . . .

Jeff reached behind him for the birch broom in the corner. If he could use it to knock the scythe aside . . .

But Dan's reaction was the most surprising of all. He sat down on the bed and clapped politely. "Very dramatic, Mr. Fillmore. A touch of the mad gardener in *Night Must Fall*. I suppose we're all going to finish up with our heads in hat boxes?"

Old Sam gaped at him. A lanky figure appeared behind him in the doorway. "Ring down the curtain, Jimmy, old chap," said Mr. Patterson cheerfully. "You've been rumbled!"

They were all sitting around amicably in the hut, drinking strong tea brewed up by Old Sam—alias Mr. James Fillmore. "It all started as a kind of joke," he was saying. "You see my wife—" He broke off. "Have you met my wife?"

Liz nodded sympathetically.

"The thing is, she hated me spending so much time at this place. She knows I don't need to, really, the business more or less runs itself, especially with old Harry here in charge." He shuddered. "She used to come down here and *get* me, drag me away to some cocktail party, or another ghastly session with her pet interior decorator. Dammit, I *like* it here, I like just puttering around the place and chatting to the customers."

"So you invented Old Sam?" said Dan.

"That's right. Harry here was in on it, of course, but I fooled the staff. I put on the disguise and turned up here with a letter of introduction from myself, and Harry took me on. That way I could spend as much time here as I liked. I'd tell my wife I was off on a business trip, and if she did turn up here looking for me, all she'd see is some old tramp puttering about." He sighed. "Trouble is, I overdid it, stayed away a bit too long, and she reported it to the police. I didn't dare come back, I'd have felt such a fool when it all came out."

"So you got stuck as Old Sam?"

"That's right. I just settled in here, and grew real whiskers to replace the false ones. It wasn't too difficult, actually, I'd always worked outdoors, so the hands and complexion were all right, and I just grew into the part." He looked almost indignantly at Dan. "How did you spot me so easily—without even seeing me?"

"I'm afraid the performance was a bit—overdone," said Dan tactfully. "Even at second hand it reeked of the footlights."

Mr. Fillmore sighed. "I suppose you're right. Let's face it, I'm a ham!"

Dan didn't contradict him. "And as for spinning Liz all those stories . . . "

Mr. Fillmore looked shamefaced. "Once I realized what she was up to, I just couldn't resist it. A chance to build up the part, you might say."

"I was just as bad," admitted Mr. Patterson. "I realized Jimmy had been spinning you a yarn, so I added one of my own. Still, you've caught us out now, and it serves us right."

"What was all that business about selling the company?" asked Liz. "Was that just a story as well?"

Mr. Fillmore shook his head. "I'm afraid not. I don't want to do it, but it seemed the only way out. Sell up, settle the money on my wife, go off and make a fresh start."

"And stay as Old Sam forever?" asked Dan. "Don't you think you'd get fed up with it?"

"I am already," admitted Mr. Fillmore gloomily. "But what's the alternative?"

"Simple," said Dan. "Get back into your own clothes, keep the beard if you like, and go home."

"What do I tell my wife? Where do I say I've been?"

"Tell her you've no idea. Say you've had a touch of amnesia, just woke up one day and found yourself at the seaside. She'll be too relieved to ask any questions."

"She really is very worried about you," added Liz gently. "I could tell when I went there. She was putting up a good front, but she was crying."

"Crying—over me?" said Mr. Fillmore, as if the idea had never occurred to him. "Good Lord. What do you think, Harry?"

"Do it," said Mr. Patterson. "Someone's got to go, and I'd sooner it was Old Sam than Jimmy Fillmore."

"Maybe I will," said Mr. Fillmore hopefully. "But what about you lot—you know the truth. I suppose you'll want to splash it in the papers—another triumph for the Irregulars."

"I think you've got the wrong idea," said Dan quietly. "Sometimes we get publicity, but we don't go out and look for it. We only got mixed up in this thing to help a friend of ours."

"What friend?"

"The policeman who was originally on the case. Detective-Sergeant Day."

"I remember him," said Mr. Fillmore. "Thin-faced young chap, very sharp. Came around asking Harry about me. I kept out of his way. He only came the once, though. Another bloke turned up yesterday, big, tough-looking feller, a bit thick. I gave him a good dose of Old Sam, and he swallowed it hook, line, and sinker."

"Anyway," said Dan. "You needn't worry about publicity from us. You go home, your wife tells the police you've turned up, and that's the end of it."

As they filed out of the hut, Mr. Fillmore asked, "What happened to that first detective anyway?"

"We're not sure," said Dan. "We're hoping to hear very soon."

As they walked to their bikes Liz asked. "*Are* we hoping to hear about Happy soon, Dan?"

"I hope so—by tomorrow, if we're lucky."

"I suppose you've cleared up that problem as well," said Jeff resignedly.

"Not yet. But we've made a start."

Mickey planted himself in front of Dan. "Come on, Robbo, not another step till you tell me."

"There's not much I can tell you, not yet. So far we've just been clearing the ground, you might say. It was never very likely that the jewel thief kidnapped Day, and I didn't think Mr. Fillmore'd got him tucked away either. We always knew the truck hijackers were the most likely candidates. As soon as Summers gets his hands on them, there's a good chance he'll find Happy as well."

"And when does that happen?"

"Tomorrow," said Dan firmly. "So don't ask me any more questions till then." He looked thoughtfully at Liz. "Didn't you say your mum was doing a few jobs for that *London— Now!* program?"

"Yes, they've just taken her on as a free-lance researcher." Liz's mother was a free-lance journalist, and *London—Now!* was a television news program with a reputation for good old-fashioned scoops.

"Is your mum home, Liz—right now, I mean?"

"I think so. She was working at home when I came out."

Dan swung a leg over his bike. "Why don't we all go around and see her? If those *London—Now!* people are as bright as they're supposed to be, I could do her a bit of good. And I could *show* you what's happening about the hijackers, instead of just telling you."

10 THE HIJACK

At six o'clock on the following evening, all four Irregulars, plus Dan's parents, were lined up in front of the big color TV in his sitting room.

At six o'clock the *London—Now!* credits came on, and after showing items about the housing shortage, the tax increases, and a defaulting financier called Santos who seemed to have vanished with several millions of other people's money, the screen showed a picture of a plain blue truck driving along the motorway. The picture was taken from behind, obviously by a camera mounted in a following car.

Liz's mum's voice came over the picture. "Now here's an item of which we're really rather proud," she said brightly. "An attempted truck hijacking, filmed as it happened. This truck is really a disguised security van and the hijackers believe it to be filled with a cargo of used bank notes on their way for destruction. As you'll see in a moment, they've set up a diversion."

The screen showed a man in the uniform of a motorway policeman waving down the truck.

The truck pulled off the road, and two more cars appeared, hemming it in.

Stocking-masked men jumped out, the driver was dragged from the cab, and two men jumped in, obviously preparing to drive it away.

The voice-over said, "However, as you can see, the thieves' information was rather unreliable."

The back door of the truck flew open, a number of policemen jumped out and swarmed all over the hijackers.

A police van drew up, the criminals were bundled inside, and police van and truck drove away. The whole thing was over in a matter of minutes, and the motorway traffic flowed on its way as if nothing had happened.

Dan's father leaned forward and switched off the set. "I don't suppose you kids could be mixed up in all that?"

"Don't be silly, dear," said Dan's mother. "They just wanted to see it because Liz's mother was doing the commentary."

"Let's go up to my room, shall we?" said Dan hurriedly, and the Irregulars all trooped out before his parents could ask any more questions.

But there were plenty of questions waiting for Dan up in his room. "So *that's* why you were so long at the police station the other night," said Liz.

Mickey was jumping up and down with excitement. "Come on, Robbo, how did you swing it?"

"And what about Day?" demanded Jeff.

"All right, all right," said Dan. "I'd worked out what was

happening soon after we got Mickey out from under that truck and I'd had a chance to have a long chat with him. It was pretty obvious someone at Anderson Transport was finding out which trucks had the valuable cargoes and someone was marking them in some way."

"Even I worked that out," said Mickey. "But which someone?"

"Burton, the security man, and Jacko, the mechanic," said Dan promptly. "Burton had a license to prowl around at night. It was easy enough for him to get a key to Anderson's safe, open it during the night, and pass the information on. That thing Mickey found on the truck was a miniaturized transmitter. Jacko stuck one on all the trucks with valuable cargoes, so the hijackers could pick them out on the motorway. When you came around asking questions, Mickey, and Burton told him you were a detective, Jacko got scared and tried to get rid of you, under that truck."

"So you decided to set a trap for them?" said Jeff.

"That's right. I persuaded Anderson to put false information into his duty-list—he'd got a cargo of used bank notes to deliver. He left it in the safe overnight, Burton got the information from the list and passed it on, and Jacko marked the truck in the usual way. Meanwhile Mr. Anderson and I went around to the police and told them what we'd done. Summers was a bit skeptical, but he couldn't risk *not* setting a trap. So he did, and as you saw, it paid off. I tipped off Liz's mum, and she arranged for the camera car to be there."

"Why were Burton and Jacko so obvious about things?" asked Liz. "And why didn't Day get on to it?"

"Burton and Jacko were obvious because they're thick," said Dan. "I imagine Burton had a grudge against Anderson because he'd got on and Burton himself hadn't. He caught sight of the list one day, realized he had something worth selling, and got in touch with some professional thieves, easy enough for a security man. Jacko had a grudge over that repairs business, and he joined in. I reckon the actual thieves knew Jacko and Burton would be caught sooner or later, but they didn't care, they were just making the most of the racket while it lasted. That's why they did so many hijackings in quick succession."

Jeff said, "So you think Day did get on to them—and they got the professional crooks to put him out of the way?"

"That's what I'm hoping. Burton and Jacko will be down at the station with the thieves by now, and Fred Summers will be giving them one of his famous 'Own up, we know it all already' terrifying-type interrogations. I'm just hoping *someone* will tell him what happened to Day."

Over the next few days the Irregulars waited eagerly for news. But Dan's hopes were not to be fulfilled. Detective-Sergeant Summers' interrogation technique scored its usual success, and Burton and Jacko made lengthy and elaborate confessions, each blaming the other.

The captured hijackers, more professional and more closemouthed, refused to say anything at all, but since there was enough evidence against them anyway, the police weren't too worried.

But no one, no one at all, admitted to knowing anything about the whereabouts of Detective-Sergeant Day.

"Are you *sure*, Dan?" said Jeff. "Maybe they just don't want to own up. If Day wasn't kidnapped bur murdered . . ." It was several days later, and they were discussing the case in Dan's room.

Dan shook his head. "I had a long chat with Fred Summers this morning. He said he sprung the business about Day on all of them, and he swears they were genuinely astonished. Anyway, I just won't believe Happy's been murdered. It just doesn't seem *likely* to me. Burton and Jacko wouldn't dare, *and* they'd be too thick to get away with it. And the real professionals just wouldn't take the risk. You don't knock off coppers in this country. It's considered unprofessional. They might have risked a kidnapping, stowing him away for a while until they could squeeze in a few more hijackings, but not murder. . . ."

"Then what do we do now?" asked Jeff despairingly. "You said it had to be tied up with one of the crimes in Day's book, but we've solved all of them now and—"

Dan leaped to his feet. "No, we haven't!"

"Haven't what?"

"Solved all of them. There's one more crime in the book— failure to give due precedence."

"You said that only means not stopping on a zebra crossing!"

"That's right."

"You're not telling me someone kidnapped a detective-sergeant just to avoid being had up for a traffic offense?"

Dan produced his favorite Sherlock Holmes quotation. " 'When you have eliminated the impossible, whatever remains, however improbable, must be the truth.' Don't you see, Jeff—we've eliminated the impossible. It wasn't Bruno the jewel thief, the man who disappeared, *or* the hijackers. So it's *got* to be the man who didn't stop on the zebra. It's *got* to be!"

Snatching up the book, Dan clattered down the stairs, Jeff close behind him, and ran to the phone in the kitchen. A few minutes later he was talking to Detective-Sergeant Summers. "Listen, Fred, this is urgent. Did Day report a traffic offense before he disappeared?" There was a brief pause, then Dan said, "Nothing in the book. You're sure? Good. Now listen, take down this car number." He read it out. "Find out who it belongs to, and ring me back right away. Look, don't give me that guff about confidential information. Who's the star of the hijacking arrests then? I should think so!" Dan slammed down the phone.

"*He didn't report it, Jeff.* The note's in his rough book, but not in his fair copy. Don't you see what that means? The offense must have occurred when he was on his way home. His proper notebook is at the station, and he wouldn't trail all the way back for a minor traffic offense. He meant to report the crime and put it in the book next day. But someone made sure he never got a chance!"

"What someone?"

"We should know that in a moment."

Dan had to pace about the kitchen for a good ten minutes before the phone rang again. He snatched it up. "Yes, okay, hang on." He began scribbling frantically on a note pad. "No, I'm not sure if I'm on to anything yet, I'll get back to you." Again he slammed down the phone. "The car was a Jag—registered not to Domingues but to a Mr. Marko Santos."

"Swindler Santos?" said Jeff incredulously. "That bloke who ran that chain of fraudulent companies? He's supposed to have cleared off to South America with his loot."

"When?" demanded Dan.

"I'm not sure. Over a week ago. The police were hunting him for ages until he got away."

Dan slammed a fist into his palm. "But he didn't, did he? He let everyone think he'd cleared off, then stayed here under cover, probably to wind up a last few shady deals. Maybe some crisis cropped up, so he had to stay. So, he's bowling along one night happily counting his stolen millions, when he nearly runs down poor old Happy on a zebra. And what does he do? He daren't produce his driving license, so he says he's forgotten it, and gives a false name!" Dan strode about the kitchen, building up a chain of lightning deductions. "Happy identifies himself as a copper, takes down the details, and lets him go, telling him to report to the station with his license next day. Happy goes off— and Santos realizes the car is registered in his real name! When he doesn't turn up at the station, Happy will check up—and realize who it was who nearly ran him down!"

"Hang on," said Jeff feebly. Dan seemed to be reeling off the story as if he'd actually been there.

"It fits, Jeff. It all fits! So Santos realizes he has to shut Happy up *before* he can report the offense. He gets in touch with some criminal pals, has Happy lured out and kidnapped. Next day he fixes up that faked safe-deposit business so the cops will think Happy's just a crooked cop on the run."

"There you are then," said Jeff. "You've solved the case.

All we need now is one minor detail. Exactly *where* is this bloke Santos keeping Happy locked up?"

"That shouldn't be too hard," said Dan calmly.

"Well, it seems to have been a bit too much for the police, doesn't it?"

"Ah, but they've stopped looking, haven't they? You said yourself, they think he's left the country. Only we know he hasn't!" Dan began pacing up and down. "Research, that's what we need now. Come on, Jeff!"

"Where to?"

"Local library. They keep back numbers of the papers. We need to know a bit more about Mr. Marko Santos."

They found plenty about Mr. Santos in the papers. The stories traced his sudden appearance on the city scene, no one quite knew from where, and the series of brilliant financial wheelings and dealings, the takeovers and stock and share manipulations that made him an instant millionaire. Then there were the increasing rumors of doubts that all was not well with the Santos empire. A minor clerk, caught out in some petty swindle, had panicked and talked, exposing shady dealings that involved the entire company. The Fraud Squad and the Inland Revenue had begun discreet investigations, and one discovery had led to another until the whole of Santos' financial network began to unravel.

The story was very complex, but it soon became clear that vast sums of money had vanished from the accounts of companies owned by Mr. Santos. Soon after that, something else emerged—Mr. Santos, it seemed, had vanished as well, coolly catching a plane to Brazil at the very instant the police were about to arrest him.

"No extradition treaty with Brazil," said Jeff. "He can sit on the beach and chat with that Great Train Robber chap."

"I doubt it," said Dan. "If he's on a beach, it's a lot nearer than Brazil!" He was studying an article in the paper. Jumping up, he used the library photocopier, handed the papers back to the puzzled assistant, and turned to Jeff. "Come on, let's go and round up the others. We're off to the seaside!"

11 THE RESCUE

A couple of hours later, after some frantic telephoning, all four were sitting in a train bound for the east coast, dragged along in the wake of Dan's enthusiasm like three tails on a single kite.

As the train pulled out of Liverpool Street, Liz had a sudden sense of familiarity. "You realize we've done this before—when we were looking for Sammy Price—on our very first case!"

They sat silent for a moment, remembering the trip down to the Essex estuary, to the lonely island where they'd been just in time to prevent a murder. Liz hoped they'd be as lucky this time.

"Don't tell me this mad millionaire keeps his yacht on Oyster Creek Island," said Mickey. "That'd be too much of a coincidence!"

Dan grinned. Oyster Creek Island was a saucer-shaped lump of mud with a few rotting houseboats, as unlikely a place for a yacht as you could imagine. "No, but he does keep it in the marina, a few miles away."

"How do you know?"

"I read it in the papers! Before he had his bit of trouble with the law, old Santos used to be in all the gossip columns. I've even got a clipping." Dan fished the photostat from his pocket and passed it around. It showed a darkly handsome man in flannels, yachting cap, and blazer, leaning over the rail of a sleek black yacht, with the usual gorgeous blonde beside him. The caption read, "Well-known yachtsman Marko Santos and friend aboard Mr. Santos' oceangoing yacht *Jolly Roger* moored at the new Oyster Creek Marina."

Jeff studied the clipping skeptically. "That's all very well, but this was before he got in trouble. How do we know the boat's still there? It may have been moved, or seized and auctioned."

Dan said, "You don't appreciate the essential fairness of British justice, Jeff. It's true that a number of companies he controlled have been found to have their assets sold off and their bank accounts emptied, that the police and the Inland Revenue and about a million shareholders are all baying after his blood, and that Mr. Santos is believed to have taken an urgent trip to South America for his health—but so far he hasn't actually been convicted of any crime. Until he is, and until all the proper procedures have been gone through, his town house, his country estate, his holiday cottage, his cars and yacht will be left undisturbed."

"We don't know Happy's on the yacht, though, do we?" argued Jeff. "He could just as well be in one of those other places."

"In a house in Mayfair, with the butler looking after him? Or down in Surrey with all the neighbors watching the

Santos house like well-bred hawks? No, it's the yacht, Jeff; it's *got* to be!"

"That yachting place is crowded enough, from what I remember," said Mickey.

"Only relatively. There's quite a bit of water between the boats, and I'll bet Santos is on a pretty isolated mooring. You can see who's coming when you're on a boat—and make arrangements to receive them."

Dan settled back in his seat, serenely confident that he was right. He didn't expect the others to understand. He didn't fully understand himself. Sometimes his mind seemed to take off on its own, working in a kind of overdrive, building one deduction on another with lightning speed. It had happened to him in the kitchen that morning, and whether it was logical deduction or just plain guesswork, Dan had never known that particular sensation to mislead him. Happy would be on Marko Santos' yacht because he had to be, and that was that.

The journey followed the same course as the one Liz remembered. They got off the Southend train at a little market town and changed onto a local diesel that seemed almost like a toy railway. The little train chugged through the flat green fields, stopping at tiny local stations where no one seemed to get on or off. Soon they came within sight of the river. As they came closer, they saw white sails gliding slowly through the fields, as though the ships were sailing on land.

They arrived at last, piled off the train, and walked down the long straggling High Street to the waterfront. This time when they reached it they turned left, not right, toward the yachting marina, which was in the fancier, more boating part of the town. The waterfront was lined with boatyards, ships chandlers, picturesque pubs, cafés, and antique shops. Dan led them toward the big marina on the edge of the town, at the point where the river widened out into open sea. On this huge area of open water, boats were moored, hundreds of them in row upon row, boats of every conceivable shape and size—motor yachts, catamarans, deep-sea cruisers, sailing vessels, and even the odd working fishing boat.

They stopped on the steps of the magnificent yacht club, and Liz gave a sigh of despair. "Talk about needles and haystacks."

"Straws and haystacks, more like," said Mickey. "How are we going to sort out one boat out of that lot?"

"If you don't know—ask," said Dan cheerfully. At that moment a stately old yachtsman was descending the steps of the yacht club. Dan went up to him, touched an imaginary cap, and said politely, "Forgive me for troubling you, sir. . . ."

The old yachtsman glared suspiciously at him, bright-blue eyes gleaming in his brick-red face. He didn't approve of modern children. Spent all their time skateboarding, mugging old ladies, and listening to appallingly loud rock 'n' roll music. However, this seemed to be an unusually polite specimen. He gave a noncommittal grunt, whiffing his snow-white mustache.

"We're looking for a yacht called the *Jolly Roger*, sir. It belongs to a Mr. Marko Santos."

The old man's eyes lit up. "The scoundrel should never have been admitted to the club. I told the committee, but did they listen to me? Oh, no. Let in anyone these days if they've got the money." He rambled on like this for quite some time.

Dan listened politely until he ran down and then said, "I'd be grateful if you could point out the yacht to me, sir."

The old boy grabbed Dan's arm in a gnarled old hand and led him to the top of the steps. "You see that blue-and-white catamaran at the far end of the moorings? The *Jolly Roger* lies just beyond it. Can't really see it from here."

"Thank you, sir. You don't happen to know if there's anyone on board?"

"Some sort of scruffy-looking caretaker feller, I think. See him rowing in for supplies occasionally. Santos will have to be expelled, of course, can't have foreign criminals in the club."

The old boy made it sound as if British criminals woud be perfectly all right, thought Dan. "Thank you very much, sir," he said, and led the others away.

They walked past the front of the yacht club and along the seawall. Dan kept the blue-and-white catamaran firmly in sight, and as they moved along, a black shape began peeping out from behind it. By the time they had rounded a curve in the seawall, the sinister black *Jolly Roger* was fully in view.

They sat down on the seawall and looked longingly at the ship, separated from them by about a quarter of a mile of water. Mirror-smooth sunlight danced off the ripples, glinted from polished hulls and gleaming brasswork. The bows of the black ship were pointing out to sea. It looked poised for a getaway, thought Dan. It was easy to imagine it slipping silently away one moonless night. Not that Santos would sail it to South America, presumably. But it would be easy enough to slip across to one of the French ports, and from there . . .

It was Mickey who asked the inevitable question. "What do we do now, Dan?"

"We wait. Watch and wait." Dan sat down and took a pair of binoculars out of his rucksack. Mickey produced a packet of sandwiches. "Might as well have a bite to eat then," he said philosophically.

They all produced their supplies and had a picnic there on the seawall. It was a pleasant spot, with the blue sunlit water stretching in front of them, the forest of yachts to their right, and the open sea stretching into the misty distance on their left. There was the boom of a cannon from the yacht club, and a fleet of white-sailed dinghies swarmed over the open water like giant butterflies.

Dan ate abstractedly, his eyes fixed on the black ship as if willing something to happen.

Suddenly he dropped his apple and snatched up the binoculars.

"Something happening?" asked Liz.

"I think someone just came up on deck. Yes, there he is, bloke in jeans and a striped jersey. He's going down the ladder to a dinghy . . . here he comes."

They all stared at the little rowboat as it moved away from the black ship, turned parallel to the shore, and rowed past them toward the town. Dan put the binoculars to his eyes again and studied the man at the oars. He gave a sudden sigh of satisfaction and passed the binoculars to Jeff. "Take a look at him, Jeff."

Jeff looked. The man was lean and dark, with a stubble of beard. "What about him?"

"Don't you know who he is?"

"Santos' caretaker, I suppose."

"Caretaker be blowed. That's Marko Santos in person! This is his hideout."

"He wouldn't dare," gasped Liz. "Come down here, when everyone's looking for him?"

"Why not? Dress up scruffy, grow a bit of a beard, stay away from the smart crowd at the yacht club—they've only seen him in posh yachting rig, remember. It'd work just because no one would think he'd dare. I bet he sent the real caretaker Domingues abroad on his own passport, to lay a false trail. He lies low here and leaves on the Domingues passport when he's ready," Dan laughed. "You've got to admire his nerve, haven't you? Look at the way he called his boat the *Jolly Roger*. He was telling everyone he was a pirate all along!"

"Are we going after him?" asked Jeff.

"Yes, but slowly, and at a distance. Pack up the picnic. Act naturally, as if we'd just decided to go. Then stroll along the wall after the boat."

They walked along the seawall, following the boat, and saw it turn into the shore and move up to one of the jetties that lined the waterfront. They saw the man in the striped jersey moor the boat and stroll along one of the alleyways that led toward the center of the town. There was an empty duffel bag over his shoulder.

"Gone shopping," guessed Dan. "Come on, now's our chance." He led them along the seawall down to the jetty and up to the dinghy. "In you get. Mickey at the front, Liz at the back. Jeff, you and I will take an oar each."

Before they knew what was happening they were in the boat, Dan had cast off, and they were moving slowly across the water toward the black ship.

"Dan, are you sure this is a good idea?" protested Liz.

"Can't think of a better one. We need a boat to get to the ship, and we want Santos out of the way. Talk about killing two birds . . ."

The little boat was overloaded with four of them, and they made pretty slow progress. Dan and Jeff heaved like a couple of galley slaves, and the *Jolly Roger* came in sight at last.

"There she is," yelled Mickey. "Heave ho, me hearties."

"Shut up, you idiot," gasped Dan. "There may be a full crew aboard, for all we know."

They moored the dinghy to the bottom of the ladder and climbed on board. The decks were empty and silent, and the masts lay along the decks, sails furled around them.

"It's like a *ghost* ship," whispered Mickey.

Liz nodded. "The *Marie Celeste*!"

Dan moved silently along the deck to a hatchway, lifted it, and climbed down a short ladder. They followed and found themselves in an oak-paneled, luxuriously carpeted corridor. "Talk about a floating hotel," whispered Jeff. At the far end of the corridor an open door gave onto the luxuriously fitted main salon, all mahogany and brass. There were doors opening off the corridor to left and right. The first showed a little cabin, with bunk, table, desk, chair, and washbasin. The second door gave onto an identical cabin— or almost identical. There was one addition.

Happy Day lay sleeping peacefully in the bunk. His clothes were rumpled, and he had a stubble of beard—everyone was bearded in this case, thought Liz fleetingly—but apart from that, he looked remarkably well.

Dan shook him gently by the shoulder, and Day opened his eyes. "There you are, young Robinson," he said, without any great surprise. "Knew you'd turn up in the end—what took you so long?"

"Sorry, Happy, we got a bit sidetracked," said Dan gently. "Can you walk?"

"I doubt it," said Day ruefully. "Take a look at my ankle."

Dan pulled back the blanket and saw that Day's left ankle was handcuffed to the brass rail that ran around the edge of the bunk. "Don't worry, we'll soon get that off," said Dan. "There must be tools somewhere."

Day grinned weakly. "You'll still have to carry me, I'm afraid. Marko gave me something to keep me quiet. I'm liable to nod off at any minute. Nice to see you again, though, Dan. . . ." Day closed his eyes and went peacefully to sleep.

Dan frowned—they were by no means out of trouble. How on earth could they get an unconscious Day down the ladder and into the dinghy? If he slipped and went into the water while he was unconscious . . . Maybe they should send someone ashore to get help. But would anyone believe them? And there was still Marko Santos somewhere on the loose.

Dan heard a bumping on the side of the ship and ran to the hatchway. He climbed out on deck, just in time to see Santos climbing over the side.

12 THE PIRATE

Santos was dripping wet. It was quite clear what had happened. He'd gone back to his dinghy, found it missing, realized something was wrong, and swum out to the ship to deal with it. A man of action, Mr. Santos.

Dan faced him. "You might as well give up, Mr. Santos," he said.

Santos' eyes widened at the mention of his own name. "You know who I am then?" The voice was deep and pleasant, with only the slightest trace of a foreign accent. "Who are you?"

"Friends of Detective-Sergeant Day."

Santos looked even more astonished as Jeff, Liz, and Mickey climbed out on deck. "Ah, yes, the famous Baker Street Irregulars. He has told me all about you, you know. Mr. Day and I have had many interesting talks. We have become quite good friends."

"Do you usually keep your friends handcuffed to their beds?" said Liz indignantly.

120

"An unfortunate necessity. I need one or two more days in England to wind up my affairs, to realize *all* my assets, and then I assure you, Mr. Day will be able to return home safe and sound—and so will you."

"You surely don't imagine you're going to keep *us* here?"

"My dear young lady, I'm afraid there's no alternative. It will be company for Mr. Day; you can discuss all your old cases. There's plenty of room, plenty of supplies. You'll be very comfortable, I assure you."

"It won't work, you know," said Liz. "For one thing the police know where we are. They'll be here any minute."

Santos stared hard at her, and to her helpless annoyance she felt herself beginning to go red. "I wonder," he said thoughtfully. "After all, if you suspected I was holding Mr. Day here, you could simply have informed the police. Instead you chose to come down and check up yourselves. So you were not quite sure, eh? And perhaps you wanted all the glory of the rescue for yourselves? No, I think you told no one. And I shall just have to gamble that I am right." He advanced toward them. "So, if you will kindly go back down the hatch, I will do my best to make you comfortable."

"Spread out, all of you," ordered Dan. "Stay as far apart as you can; he can't catch us all."

White teeth flashed in Santos' bearded face. "Oh, but I can. One by one I can catch you and knock you out and take you below. Even the young lady, if I must. Why not come now and save a good deal of unpleasantness?"

The Irregulars spread out on the deck in a semicircle. No one moved.

"No?" said Santos regretfully. "Then the leader first, I think." He sprang toward Dan.

Dan stood his ground, relying on the knowledge of judo that had helped him in similar encounters. As Santos reached for him, he dodged and tried for an over-the-shoulder throw. . . .

Santos avoided his grip with ease, grabbed Dan by sleeve and lapel, and suddenly it was Dan who went flying through the air. He managed to land on his shoulder and roll onto his feet, but the experience left him badly shaken.

"I too have studied judo," said Santos gently.

Jeff tapped Santos on the shoulder. "What about boxing?" As Santos turned, Jeff launched a mighty straight left at his nose. Santos moved his head slightly, the fist whizzed by, and he tapped Jeff lightly on the point of the jaw. Jeff staggered back a few paces and sat down hard.

"Boxing, too!" said Santos.

There was a bucket standing by the hatch cover. Suddenly Mickey darted toward it, snatched it up, leaped on top of the hatch cover, and slammed the bucket down over Santos' head. "How about rough-and-tumble, mate?"

Half choked by dirty water, Santos staggered across the deck, roaring with rage. "Quick," yelled Mickey. "Over the side with him!" He started shoving Santos backward, Liz joined in, and Dan and Jeff came to help. Between the four of them they whizzed Santos across the deck to the safety rail at the side of the deck and shoved hard.

The rail caught Santos behind the knees and he toppled over backward, parting company with the bucket and hitting the water with a tremendous splash.

Jeff gasped and rubbed his chin. "A bit unsporting, Mickey—but effective!"

"Partly effective," said Dan. He pointed and they looked over the side. The current had carried the flailing Santos some way past the boat, but he had recovered himself and was swimming back toward it.

"Dan, what are we going to do?" said Jeff urgently. "We'll never get Day free and into the boat with him jumping on us."

Dan looked around for inspiration—and suddenly he found it. "We don't need a boat to go ashore in. We're already on a boat, Jeff; you stand by to cast off fore, and I'll go aft. Liz, see if you can get the engines started, Mickey stand by to repel boarders."

"You're not going to try and move this thing?" yelled Mickey. "It's as big as the *Queen Elizabeth*."

"It's all right," said Dan. "We're not going far. Steer straight for the shore, Liz, the minute you get her moving."

"Right!" said Liz and dashed for the wheelhouse.

Dan went to the mooring cables at the back of the boat, Jeff to the front.

Mickey looked around for a weapon and spotted the mop that had been in the bucket. He grabbed it and whirled around, just as Santos' face appeared over the side.

Mickey leveled the mop and charged, like a knight with a lance. The mop took Santos full in the face, and he fell back off the ladder, hitting the water with a splash for the second time.

In the wheelhouse, Liz was studying the controls. She could drive a car pretty well, and after all, an engine was an engine. . . . She pressed what she hoped was the starter. It was—and the engines began throbbing slowly.

She waved to Dan, who cast off his mooring. Dan waved to Jeff, who promptly did the same.

Liz threw the engines into forward and grabbed the wheel. The great yacht swung around and headed for the shore with terrifying speed.

Suddenly Liz realized—there are no brakes on a boat. She put the engines into reverse, but it was too late.

Narrowly missing the yacht-club jetty, the bows of the *Jolly Roger* struck the muddy bank and slid up the seawall. For one delirious moment it looked as if the yacht would go sailing across the fields.

Then she stuck hard, tilted over sideways, with an impact that knocked the Irregulars off their feet—and threw Marko Santos into the water for the third time.

With a gasp of relief, Liz switched off the engines and sat down on the wheelhouse floor.

There was the most appalling fuss after that. As Mickey said, it was like Dunkirk. From all over the estuary, little boats set out to the rescue.

For a while the Irregulars were nearly lynched by irate yachtsmen, who thought they'd taken a ship for a bit of joyriding, but Dan's calm explanation and the sight of the pale young policeman handcuffed to the bunk soon put a stop to all that.

The police appeared, and Day was released and carried ashore on a stretcher, then whizzed off to hospital.

Dan and Jeff and Liz and Mickey were shipped off to the

police station and questioned by an angry policeman who didn't understand half they were saying and didn't believe the other half.

For a while it looked as if they'd spend a night in the cells. Luckily Day revived in the hospital and made a statement exonerating his rescuers. Instantly converted from villains to heroes, the Irregulars were showered with praise, given tea and bacon sandwiches, and finally driven home in triumph in a police car.

Mickey thought that was the best part of all. "We had the siren on *all the way*," he told his awestruck friends later. "And I'll swear we touched ninety on the motorway!"

In all the noise and fuss and confusion, something, or rather somebody, passed unnoticed. By the time anyone thought to look for him, Marko Santos had slipped quietly away. Dan alerted the police and they made an intensive search of the area. But no trace of the missing man was ever found.

"Can't say I'm sorry, really," said Day, a few days later. He was now installed back in his office, and Dan was an honored visitor. "Quite a likable bloke, old Marko, in his way."

"Apart from little weaknesses like stealing money and kidnapping policemen, that is! How did he get hold of you anyway?"

Day's story confirmed most of Dan's theories. "I'm trudging wearily home from late shift at the station, right, and this Jag comes screaming around the corner and nearly knocks me flying off the zebra crossing. Naturally this makes me a bit ratty, so I flash the warrant card and tell the driver he's about to be done for failing to give due precedence. He spins me some yarn about speeding to his sick mother's bedside. I ask to see his license, which he hasn't got. So I take down the name he gives, Domingues, and the car number, tell him to report at the station next morning with the license and make a statement, and let him go. It's not till I'm back home having a cuppa at Mrs. H's that the penny drops, and I realize why he looked familiar. We've got his picture up at the station! So there I am wondering what to do about it when the phone rings, and there's old Marko. Says he's seen the error of his ways and wants to turn himself in to me personally. Which of course would be a very nice arrest to have on my record. So I trot out all innocent, the Jag's waiting in the street, and Marko ushers me inside, pulls a gun on me, knocks me cold with some kind of blackjack, and the next thing I know it's life on the ocean wave."

"Did you tell him your name when you stopped him?" asked Dan.

Day nodded. " 'I am Detective-Sergeant Day,' I said. That shook him."

"Do you have a separate phone at the house?"

"There's two phone numbers, one for the Hoskins, one for me in my room. Just had it put in. I get calls all hours, and Mrs. H got cheesed off."

"And you're in the telephone book?"

Day nodded again. "Why?"

"That's how he got your number. You told him your name, he followed you home for the address, then looked you up in the book."

Day said, "I expect you're right. Anyway, it all got a bit

hazy after that, till you turned up and staged your ship-wreck," Day sighed. "Trouble is, I've got all me old cases to catch up on now." He began rooting through his files.

Dan coughed. "I wouldn't worry too much about that if I were you, Happy," he said gently. "As a matter of fact, I think you'll find your desk is pretty clean. . . ."

"The underlying theme of the books might be called kids' lib," says author Terrance Dicks of his Baker Street Irregulars series. "Children are smarter than anyone gives them credit for."

In addition to authoring the Irregulars series, Mr. Dicks has published more than forty other books for young people, been an advertising copywriter and TV and radio scriptwriter, and has edited material for the BBC. Perhaps his best-known work is as scriptwriter for the TV science-fiction series *Doctor Who*. He is married and the father of three sons; he lives in London.